THE EYE OF THE STORM

OSKAR KÄLLNER • KARL JOHNSSON

PAPERCUTZ

CHILDREN OF THE PHOENIX
THE EYE OF THE STORM

Logo design - David Reyes
Cover design - Karl Johnsson
Production - JayJay Jackson & Charles Pritchett
Senior Editor - Zohra Ashpari
Editor in Chief - Mike Marts

Laura Chacón - Founder
Mark London - CEO and Chief Creative Officer
Mark Irwin - Senior Vice President
Mike Marts - EVP and Editor-in-Chief
Chris Fernandez - Publisher
Stephanie Brooks - Editor
Adam Wallenta - Editor

Papercutz was founded by Terry Nantier and Jim Salicrup

PB ISBN: 9781545811337

BROCK

"Incoming message."

Arisa's voice projects into the Phoenix's bridge. The only other sound is the low background hum of the engines.

Brock turns his large lizard body in his captain's chair, ignoring the flickering hologram screens of graphs and status updates, and looks up towards the hidden speakers in the ceiling where Arisa's voice is coming from.

"Who is it from?"

"Parishvi."

Brock gets up from his chair. His feet land with a heavy thud on the ship's metal floor.

"From Parishvi? Are you sure?"

"The message is encrypted with her unique signature. Chances of forgery are negligible."

Parishvi. What could she want after all this time? He puts his hand on the captain's chair and slowly drags his claws along the metal. It had always been her sitting in this chair. She had been the one giving orders and leading the

Phoenix on mission after mission. Until that final job. The one that went so horribly wrong.

A shudder runs through his body. He hasn't thought about Parishvi in a long time and isn't prepared for the feelings it stirs up.

"Play the message," he says.

"Decryption is underway," says Arisa. "It will be ready soon. A little patience."

Brock sighs and taps his tail on the floor.

He knows that the sharp spikes leave marks, but right now, he can't bring himself to care.

The double doors to the bridge slam open and Syndra storms in. Her cheeks are flushed against her blue face and her red hair stands on end like a flame.

"A message. Can it really be true? From Parishvi?"

"Yes."

"So she wants to get in touch now?" She slams her metal hand into the wall so hard it hums. "So she couldn't leave us a message when she disappeared? One word would have been enough, just to let me know that she was alive out there."

"Well, I got a message, two years later," says Brock.

"Yes, I know! And that just makes me angrier!"

"I was her second-in-command."

"And I was her…"

Syndra trails off and brings her other hand, made of flesh and blood, to her head and massages her temple.

"I'm sorry," she says. "I just get so… How dare she get in touch now! Where has she been all these years?"

Brock raises his claw to scratch the small, soft scales under his chin.

"All she said was that she had found a somewhat primitive planet and settled there. That she had met a mate and started a family."

Brock laughs. The thought of Parishvi with a wrinkly blue baby in her arms seems utterly absurd.

"The decryption is ready," Arisa says over the speakers. "Shall I play it?"

"Yes!" exclaim Brock and Syndra simultaneously.

He gives her a stern look. After all, he is the captain. She just shrugs her shoulders.

"There's no video," says Arisa. "Playing audio now."

Parishvi's voice sounds throughout the bridge.

"Brock! I need your help. The Krao are here… I've seen at least one of their ships. There may be more. I don't know why they've come or how they found their way here. Someone must have hired them, and I don't know what their intentions are, but it can't be good for this planet. Some of my monitoring sensors disappeared yesterday. I think they've taken them… Which means they know I live here. I have to protect my family, my children." There is a pause. "Please Brock. Come as quickly as you can. And Brock, if Syndra is still on the Phoenix, or if you are in contact, tell her I'm sorry. Tell her I hope she can forgive me."

There is a click and the speakers are silent.

Brock's heart is pounding and he realizes he has been whipping his tail against the floor. Parishvi needs him. Now!

Syndra is leaning against a wall, breathing heavily. She looks up at him.

"We have to help her."

He places a hand on her shoulder and looks her straight in the eye.

"Of course."

Syndra visibly relaxes and her face softens somewhat.

"If I may have your attention," says Arisa. "The message came with coordinates to a planet. But there's something odd. The planet's solar system lies well outside the Sickle in an area that was mapped by the empire over 400 years ago."

"What's odd about that?" asks Brock.

"This planet isn't on the map."

Brock is taken aback.

"That's impossible! There must be a mistake!"

"The empire didn't make those sorts of mistakes. But still, the planet is not on the map."

Syndra puts her hands on her hips.

"What difference does that make? We still have to go there. I have a few things to say to Parishvi once I see her."

"I can imagine," Brock says with a snort. "Lucky we have no other assignments at the moment. Arisa, set the course for this planet." He glances up at the ceiling. "What's it called?"

"The inhabitants call it Earth."

"Earth?" says Syndra. "Like soil?"

"That is correct."

"So that would make them… earthlings?"

"Correct."

"As in, creatures of earth?" Syndra starts laughing. "I know they're a primitive planet, but naming it after the dirt they walk on? That's just bizarre!"

Brock gives her a look but says nothing. If he spent all his time trying to keep Syndra under control he would never get anything done.

"Hyperspace coordinates entered," says Arisa. "It's a long journey."

"Best we get going," says Brock. "Parishvi is waiting for us."

"Aye, Captain."

Space explodes into light as the Phoenix leaves the ordinary universe behind and launches into hyperspace, towards the planet known as Earth.

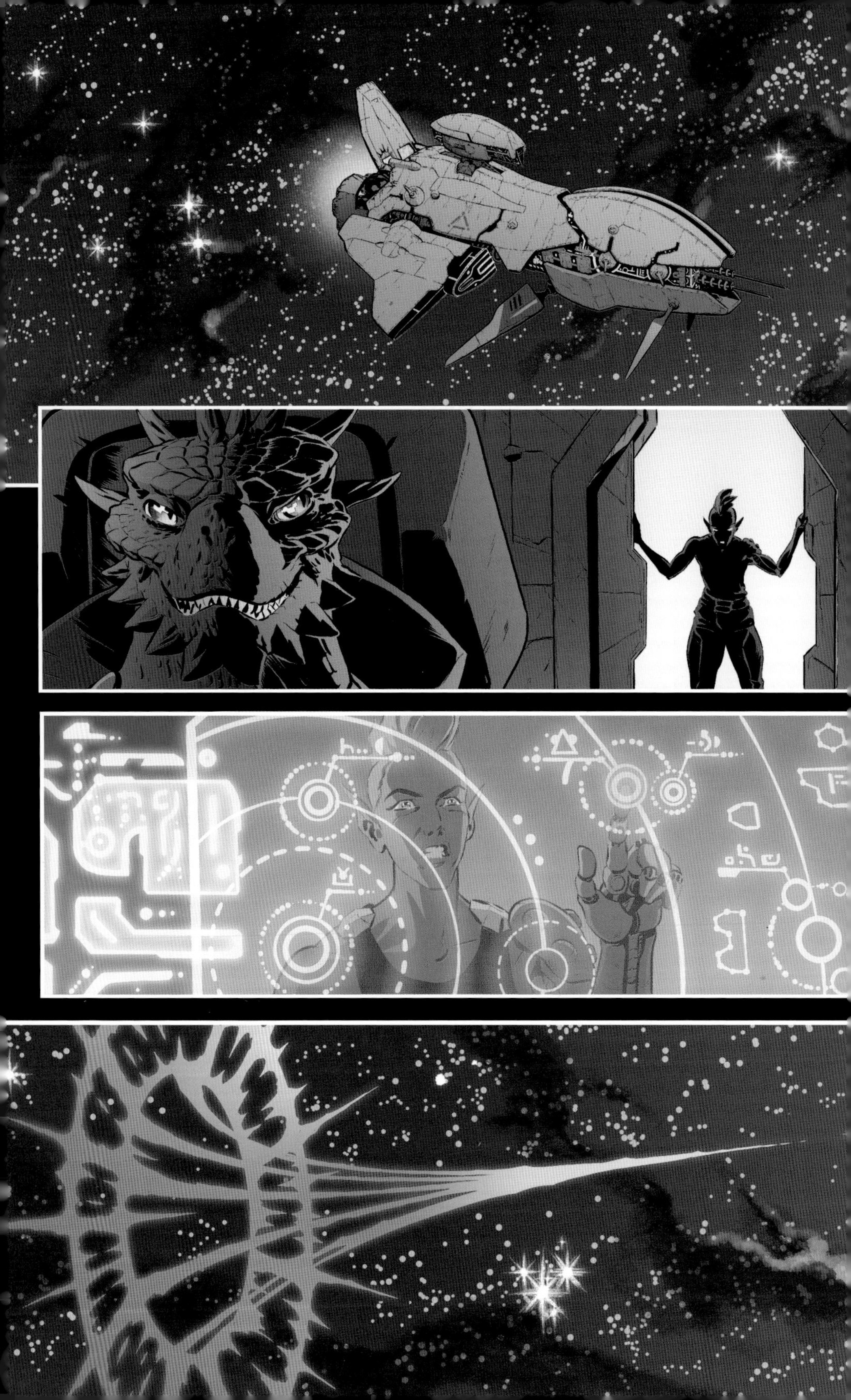

ELIAS

"OK, so you know what to do, right?" says Alice, looking at him intensely.

Elias' knees turn to jelly. He leans against the brick wall of the school and tries to calm himself down. He really doesn't want to do this. The teachers at Sunnersta school must have noticed his absence by now. They probably think he's playing hooky. Which technically he is.

"Why do I have to climb through the window? Can't you do it?"

"Oh, so you're going to distract Janet then?"

Elias knows he can't do that. He doesn't have the gift of gab like his big sister. His lies couldn't fool anyone. He might as well be transparent. Alice, on the other hand, can lie straight to people's faces and make it look easy.

"I don't know if this is such a great idea," he says.

Alice scoffs.

"It's an amazing idea! What could possibly go wrong?"

How about everything? Like what if Janet comes back and

finds him? And realizes that he doesn't even go to this school? And makes him call Dad? Dad would get angry. Very angry.

But Elias says nothing. There's no point in trying to reason with Alice once she has made up her mind about something. He tries to clear his head instead. Focus. But it doesn't work, something else is gnawing at him.

"Mom wasn't home this morning," he says.

Alice gives him a strange look.

"What's that got to do with anything?"

"Did she even come home last night?"

"I don't know."

"I tried texting and calling, but she's not picking up."

Alice looks away and says nothing. Elias gets the feeling that she's tried contacting Mom, too.

"Where do you think she is?" he says.

Alice groans.

"Do we have to talk about this right now? She probably just needed a bit of alone time after the fight. I bet she's already come home while we've been at school."

"But what if she hasn't?"

"Then she'll come home this evening."

Elias swallows, clenches his fists, and closes his eyes. In his mind's eye he can picture Mom and Dad standing on the street screaming at each other. Dad, big, angry and thunderous. Mom, with burning eyes and a voice as sharp as a knife.

They were supposed to have a cozy evening in.

He takes a deep breath. Then he feels a playful pinch on the earlobe. He opens his eyes and meets his big sister's gaze.

"Come on, bro," she says. "I need you. If you don't help me with this math test I'm in trouble. Got it? Deep trouble."

Elias stands firmly on both feet.

"OK. I'll do it."

Alice beams.

"Great. Let's go!"

Elias sneaks around the back of the school building. He's supposed to go to window number seven. Alice had checked to make sure Janet had left it open. According to Alice, teachers do this all the time during the summer. The building doesn't exactly have the best ventilation.

He crouches and scuttles quickly below the windows. One, two, three, four, five, six. He presses himself against the brick wall under the seventh and waits. He hears someone clear their throat inside. It sounds like a woman, but he can't be sure. He hears a pencil scratching against a piece of paper. Skritz ritz skritz… He starts to sweat. Where's Alice?

Just then there is a knock on the door. A hard, rapid knock He hears someone get up and opens the door, and then an older woman's voice, "Hi Alice. What's the matter?"

"It's Patrick! The other boys dragged him into the toilets in the seventh grade corridor. They're going to flush his head down the toilet! I couldn't find any of the teachers on break duty. You have to help him."

Janet lets out a deep sigh.

"I'm coming."

The door slams.

Elias immediately takes a firm grip on the window ledge, jumps and heaves himself up. The office is the size of a closet; it barely fits a desk, two chairs and two bookshelves.

Where would she keep the math tests? That was the only thing Alice had been a bit vague about. A file or folder saying "Seventh Grade Tests." Easier said than done. The shelves are full of binders and folders and papers and books, and Elias can't see what he's looking for. He runs his finger along the labels on the spines of the binders. Not here. He looks through the papers on the desk, carefully. He doesn't want the teacher to suspect anything when she comes back.

Then he sees a metal cabinet under the desk. He pulls the handle. Locked. He quickly looks through the desk drawers, and at the bottom of the top drawer he finds a small, grey steel key that looks like it might fit.

Quickly, before he can change his mind, he puts the key into the lock and turns it. Click. The cabinet opens. And there they are: the tests. In neat piles and color-coded folders on the shelf. The natural science tests are on top, the physics tests are on the side, and on the bottom shelf are the math tests. He flicks through the piles. Sixth grade, eighth grade… seventh grade!

Just then he hears a voice coming from the other side of the door. An unusually loud voice.

"How strange, I can't imagine where they've gone. But thanks for checking anyway."

Janet mumbles something, the door handle is pushed down and the door opens. Elias looks up in panic and catches Alice's eye. Janet has her back to him, but she could turn around at any second. And then they're toast. Then they are call-the-parents-toast, see-the-headmaster-toast, maybe even call-the-police-toast. Though Elias isn't sure whether the police would get involved in a case of a stolen math test.

Alice reacts immediately, whimpering in anguish and clutching her belly.

"What's the matter?" asks Janet.

"It's probably nothing, it's…"

Alice falls to the floor with a groan. Janet bends down.

"Do you need help?"

Quick as a flash, Elias snatches the top test from the seventh grade folder, crumples the pages into his pocket and closes the cabinet.

"My stomach hurts!" he hears Alice gasp as if she is going through hellish torment.

Janet could turn around at any moment. Elias doesn't dare lock the cupboard and put the key back. He gets up, takes one agile leap over the windowsill and lands out on the lawn.

Shame about the key. Still, he had no choice but to get out of there. Hopefully Janet will assume she left the key in the lock herself.

Through the window he can hear that Alice has stopped whining.

"Sorry about that," she says with a heavy sigh. "It's OK now. Must have been a cramp or something."

"Maybe I should call the school nurse?" asks Janet.

Alice's voice becomes steadier at once.

"No, I'm fine. Just a little tired. Maybe I'll skip my last class and go home."

"Yes, you do that."

Elias doesn't hear any more because he's already making his way back, crouched under the windows, towards the meeting place outside the school library.

"Did you get the test?" says Alice.

She's excited – this is her idea of fun. Elias, on the other hand, feels like a deflated balloon. He is utterly exhausted after all that stress.

"Yes," he says, and takes the crumpled papers from his pocket.

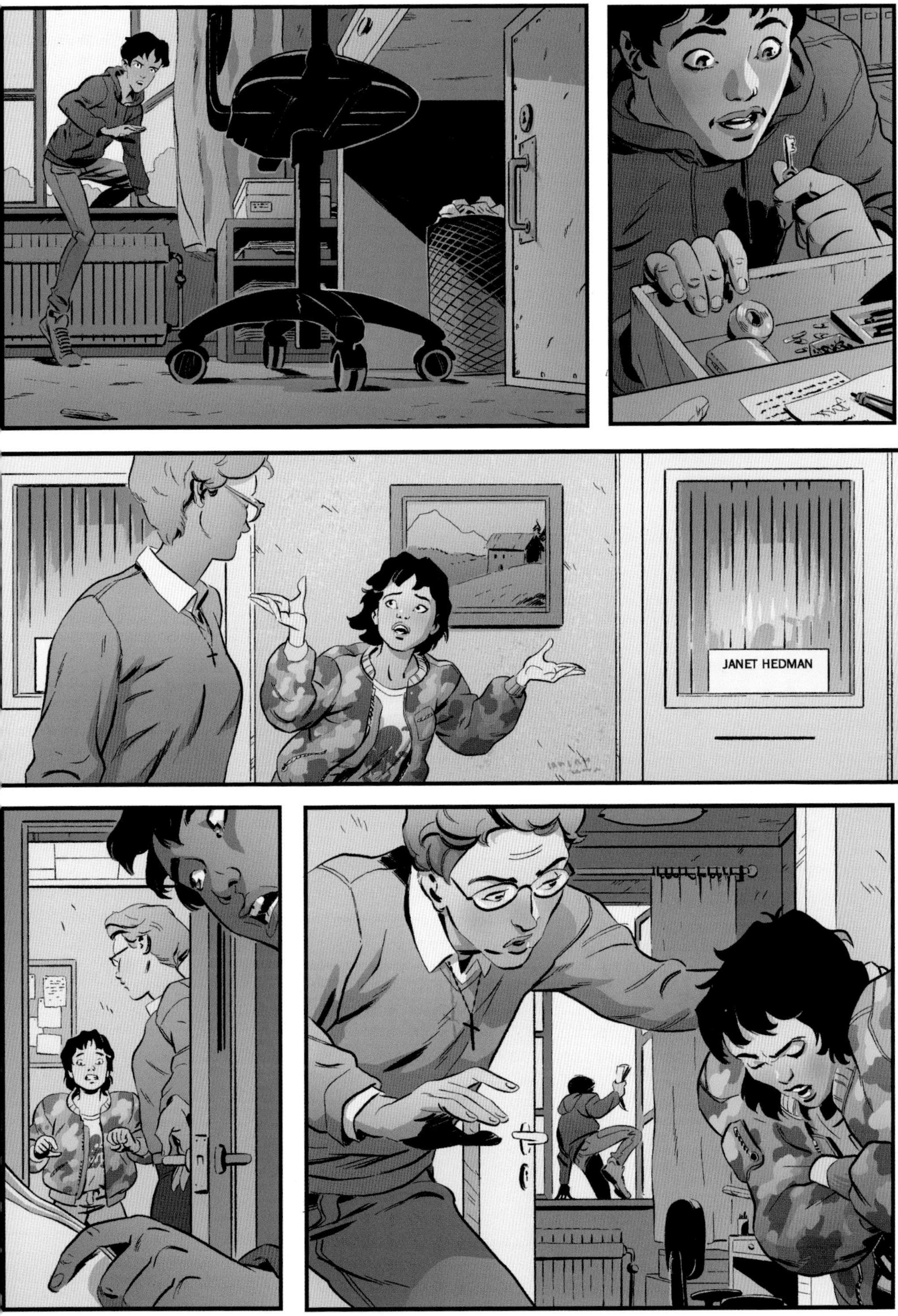
JANET HEDMAN

"Awesome!" says Alice with a triumphant laugh. "By the way, what did you think of my amazing performance? Convincing medical emergency, wasn't it?"

Elias doesn't answer. He stands quietly beside Alice as she flicks through the papers.

"But… We've already taken this test!"

Disappointment spreads across her face. "You took the wrong test! You were supposed to get the next one!"

Anger sparks inside Elias.

"Why didn't you look at the date? It's right here!" she continues.

The little spark flares up. Elias feels his cheeks warming up.

"Break in yourself next time then!" he practically screams. "I did my best!"

Alice looks at him. Then her face softens, she puts her arms around him and hugs him hard.

"Sorry. You were awesome. Like a ninja! I'm just disappointed. I'm sorry, Elias. Forgive me?"

"Stop it. You're embarrassing me."

She laughs and lets him go. He sees a few of her classmates not too far away, looking in their direction. Alice follows his gaze.

"Let them stare," she says. "Come on. Let's go home."

ALICE

Alice steers her bike into the garage driveway with Elias close behind. They have lived here for as long as she can remember, in the yellow wooden house with white trim and a black roof. It's early afternoon, but it looks like Dad is home already. His Mazda is parked on the gravel. The Volvo PV's usual spot is empty. Mom still isn't back.

There is a flutter in Alice's stomach. She doesn't know what she was expecting, but she had hoped everything would be back to normal again when they got home from school. Howling electric guitar riffs are coming from the garage.

"Come on," Elias says and starts heading in that direction.

But Alice doesn't want to. She doesn't want to talk to Dad, not after how he behaved last night. She reaches out to stop Elias but he has already gone ahead and opened the garage door.

The music stops.

"Home already?" Dad sounds a little groggy, as he usually does when he's had a bad night's sleep.

She peeks into the garage, which looks the same as ever. Storage shelves filled with junk lining the walls. There are dry oil stains on the floor from back when Dad worked evenings and nights to restore the Volvo for mom. Dad is sitting at his drum kit in the corner with his guitar in his lap. He stands up and leans on the workbench.

He is a large man with a red beard and blue eyes. He used to play guitar in a band. Alice has lost count of how many times he has told them about the time he played the Hultsfred Festival. But despite their success, the band split just a few months later. She has seen photos from that time, the old-fashioned type of photos on paper. Dad was young then and full of dreams of becoming a rock star.

"But then I might never have had you," he would say and ruffle their hair. Or at least he used to. He always used to be full of jokes and mischief, roaring with laughter with his great big beard. But Mom and Dad have been arguing more than usual lately. Dad has a bad temper and Mom isn't exactly the type to give in. She's been working really hard, always on the move, and Dad hasn't liked it. But today he just seems sad. His eyes dart anxiously between Alice and Elias.

"Have you heard from Mom?"

"No," says Elias. "Have you?"

Dad looks down.

"No. Nothing."

Anger bubbles up in Alice. She wants to scream and swear at him. If only he didn't get so angry all the time! Dad takes a step forward and holds out his arms. Elias goes immediately to hug him. Dad tries to bring Alice in, but she pushes his hand away.

CHAPTER 3

"Leave me alone!"

He looks even sadder and hugs Elias tighter. Alice turns around demonstratively and sees the new terrarium that Dad has built for her. She has always liked insects. When she was little, she could spend hours in the blueberry bushes in Lunsen forest watching the ants, beetles, and caterpillars. Last year she got a small plastic terrarium with African beetles. They are colorful, with green bodies, red legs, and white striped shells. Now Dad has built a new, bigger terrarium for her, so she can use the old one for something else, maybe a big hairy spider. Alice likes spiders.

She feels a little guilty when she looks at the glass and aluminum contraption. But Dad has let go of Elias now. Cuddle time is over.

"Have you tried calling the university? Maybe they know something?" she says.

Dad's face darkens.

"I did a while ago. They haven't seen her all day."

"Can you call the police?" asks Elias.

His eyes are red and puffy.

"The police?" says Dad. "No, she'll be home soon enough. She's just angry."

"But what if something's happened to her?" Elias insists.

Alice would rather not think about it, but something actually might have happened to Mom. She was very angry with Dad, but she would never just abandon her and Elias like this.

Alice leaves the garage. The Volvo is still glaringly absent in the driveway. She remembers the day when Dad gave Mom the car keys. She was so happy. Mom loves old cars. The Volvo has a large luggage compartment where she can put all her equipment when she has to go out and take measurements for work.

Dad and Elias follow Alice out. Their eyes also fix on the empty parking spot.

"Maybe I should call the police after all," says Dad. "Maybe they can help." He laughs a short, hollow laugh. "It's not like it can make things any worse."

ELIAS

The doorbell rings. Ding dong. Ding dong.

Outside the window, the sun is setting and its final rays cast a golden glow on the street. Elias is stretched out on the sofa balancing his tablet on his lap. A cartoon flickers on the screen. Spider-Man has just defeated Electro, but he's not out of the woods yet, because now Doctor Octopus is getting in on the action.

The doorbell rings again.

"Elias! Can you get that?" Dad calls from the basement.

He slumps further down on the sofa.

"Elias!?"

"Elias. Dad's calling you," Alice says from the kitchen.

But he has no desire to leave the comfy sofa.

He has no desire to think about anything other than how Spider-Man is going to tie Doctor Octopus's long tentacle arms together. There is a knot in his stomach and if he starts to think about the reason why, he fears the pain will become unbearable.

It rings a third time. Elias focuses on his tablet, absorbed in the skyscrapers of New York along with Spider-Man, Nova, Iron Fist and the gang. He has no intention of moving until this is all over and Mom is home again.

"Alice!" Dad yells. "Get that, would you?!"

Elias hears his big sister sigh and plonk something down by the sink with a bang, then she marches through the living room. From the corner of his eye, he sees her shake her head and toss her hair back. She always does that when she's annoyed.

"It wouldn't kill you to help, you know," she says.

Elias focuses on the tablet screen. The Hulk will show up soon. Elias knows because he has seen this episode before.

"Hulk smash," he mumbles.

"You're impossible," Alice says, going out into the hall.

The doorbell rings one more time before she opens it.

"Good evening, we're with the police. Are you Alice? We have been notified that your mother has disappeared?"

"Dad! It's the police! "Alice shouts.

Footsteps sound up the stairs from the basement and Dad appears. He almost fills the entire doorway and his blue eyes are wide with concern. Elias has Dad's eyes. Same color, same shape, same eyebrows. But other than that, everyone says he looks like his mother. The thought of this makes his stomach clench again. He focuses on the cartoon and tries not to think at all.

Spider-Man throws a sticky cobweb over Doctor Octopus's face and Elias almost laughs.

Almost.

"Hello. My name is Frida Rotenius," says one of the police officers.

"Zaid Shakir," says the other.

"Adam Johansson," says Dad.

Elias hears the police officers come inside and close the front door.

Now the Hulk has arrived. Finally!

"Where have you been?" says Dad. "I called several hours ago."

"Most people who are reported missing show up within 24 hours," says Frida. "So we don't usually come before that. In this instance we are actually a few hours early."

The policeman called Zaid steps into the living room. Elias looks up at him. He has sharp features and stubble.

"May we sit down?" he says.

Elias looks down without answering.

"Of course," says Dad as he and Frida come into the room. "Move down, boy."

But Elias doesn't want to move.

"Move down!" Dad repeats emphatically.

Elias reluctantly retreats to the corner of the sofa.

The police officers sit and Dad drops into an armchair

opposite them. Alice is hesitant and lingers in the kitchen doorway. Zaid picks up a notepad and taps a pen against his notebook.

"So… Tien Johansson. Forty-five years old. She came here from Vietnam as an exchange student in a research project fifteen years ago. You met and she stayed here in Sweden. Is that correct?"

"Yes," says Dad. "One day she came into the garage where I worked. Her car had broken down and she had no money. I fixed it in exchange for the privilege of taking her out for dinner." Suddenly he smiles and his whole face lights up. "And I never looked back. Fifteen years later and here we are with a house in Sunnersta and two wonderful kids."

"You're still a car mechanic, right?" Frida says.

Something about her tone sounds like she thinks it's the worst profession in the world. She is reading something on her phone.

"At a garage in Fyrislund?"

"That's right."

"And Tien disappeared last night?"

"Yes. She's been doing research into atmospheric phenomena at Uppsala University." Dad shrugs his shoulders slightly. "Don't ask me what exactly, I don't know anything about it. But last night she went out to set up some new measuring equipment in Lunsen. Apparently, it has to be set up quite deep in the forest to avoid light pollution from the city."

"Does she often go there to set up measuring equipment? Even in the evenings?"

"Yes, but it only used to be once a year or so. In the last few months she's been out several times a week. She said something about intensified measurement data." Dad sighs. "I don't know."

"Did anything unusual happen yesterday evening?" Frida asks. "Anything out of the ordinary?"

"No, not at all." Dad catches Elias' eye, then quickly looks over at Alice. She glares back at him. "We'd planned on having a cozy night in. She was sitting right where you are now." Dad gestures at Zaid. "But then she got a text, leapt off the sofa, ran down to the basement, and came back with some weird sort of device. Then she got straight in her Volvo and drove off."

Elias looks out the window, just like he did last night when Mom left. He had popcorn in his hand at the time, and his mouth was salty from the seasoning.

Darkness is falling across the neighborhood. A couple of headlights attract his attention. Another police car drives down the street and stops outside their house. What's it doing here? Frida just said that the police don't usually investigate disappearances within 24 hours. And now more police are here as well as Frida and Zaid? The knot in his stomach tightens. Something is wrong.

Two uniformed policemen step out of the car, cross the road to the Ingemarsson house, and ring the doorbell. The door opens and the police start talking to the woman who lives there. Elias looks over at Alice. She has also seen the other police officers. She looks even angrier.

"OK," says Zaid. "So Tien left the house and drove off in her Volvo. What did you do?"

"I…" Dad hesitates. "I drove after her."

Elias can still hear the angry voices; he can see the whole scene playing out before him. The racket out on the driveway. Mom shaking her fist at Dad, with car keys in hand, then turning around to leave. Dad grabbed her by the shoulders to try to stop her. She jerked free and hissed something at him. There was desperation on Dad's face as mom jumped into the Volvo and sped off. Dad was there looking lost, before getting into his car and disappearing after her.

"And you were driving that Mazda parked outside?" asks Zaid.

"Yes. I drove to the nature reserve at Lunsen. But her car wasn't in the car park."

"Is it possible you just didn't see it?"

"Didn't see it? It's a Volvo PV445 – a classic! Not the sort of car you miss."

"OK," Zaid says. "Then what did you do?"

"I had no idea where she'd gone, so I drove home again."

"Wait a minute," says Frida. "You left the children alone?"

Dad's face turns red.

"Yes, but they're grown now. They're fine on their own for a little while."

"Why did you follow her?" says Zaid.

"I was concerned. I wanted to talk to her."

"Couldn't you just call her?" Frida says, as if Dad were a complete idiot.

"She wasn't picking up."

"Why not?"

"How should I know?" Dad stands up angrily. "What is this? Some kind of cross-examination? I want you to find my wife! Can you do that?"

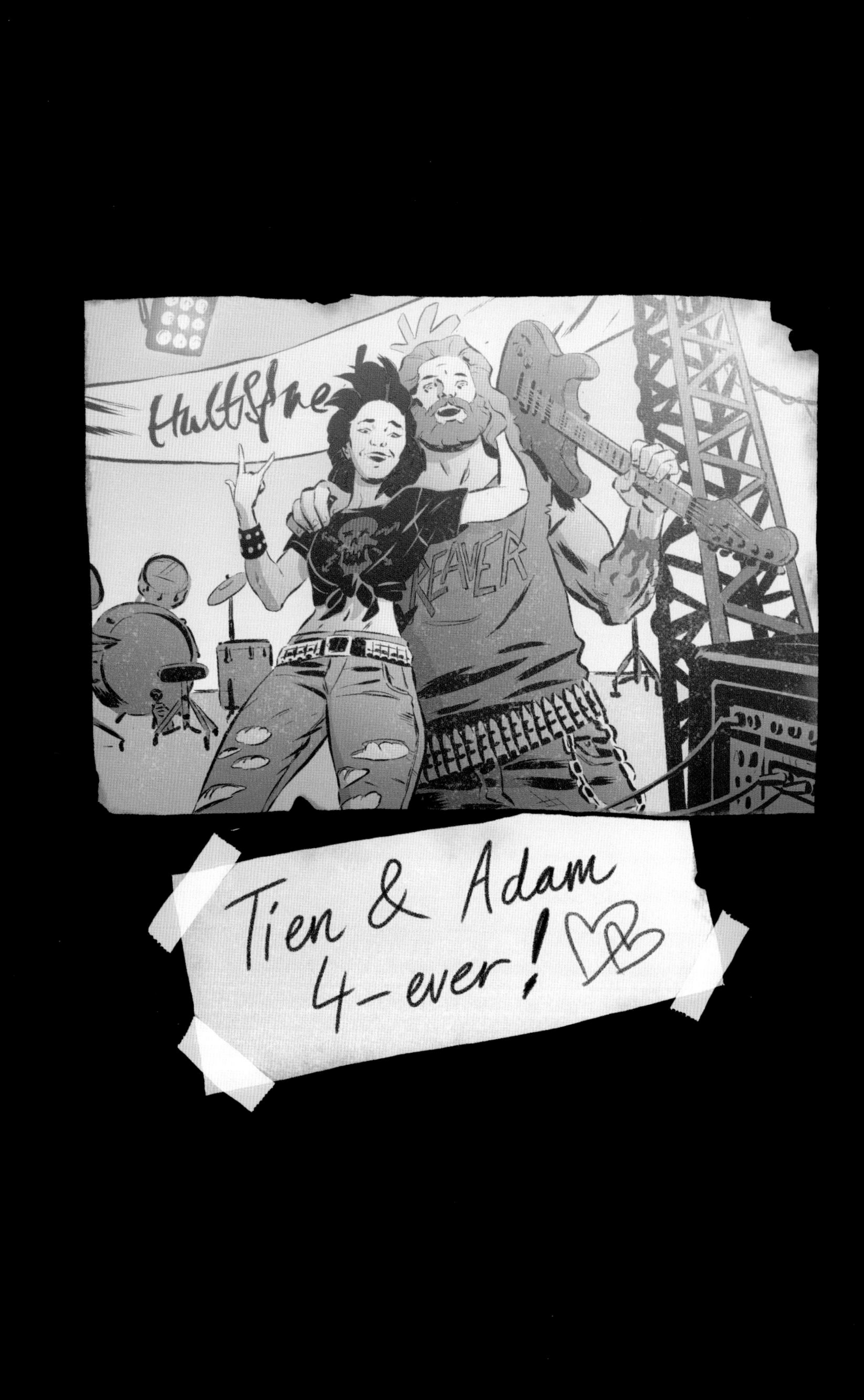
REAVER
Tien & Adam
4-ever!

ELIAS

Elias wants the ground to swallow him up. Or to run and hide in his bedroom. Dad is so embarrassing! But it feels like the sofa has a suction grip on his body and refuses to let go.

Dad's face has turned scarlet red, his chest is heaving and his hands are clenched into large fists. Elias looks down again. Spider-Man has just climbed up a crane and is making snarky comments as the Hulk attacks Doctor Octopus.

In the corner of his eye he sees Frida hold up her hands defensively. Dad takes control of his temper, sighs deeply and sits down.

"We're asking these questions because we want to find her. But in order for us to do so, you have to tell us what happened the night she disappeared."

Frida's phone beeps. She skims the message and her posture changes. She becomes stiffer, more alert.

"Some neighbors have reported a loud argument between you and Tien before she drove off," she says. "You two were standing on the street and speaking in raised voices. Is that true?"

Elias squirms in his seat. Alice explodes.

"Did you really think they wouldn't find out, Dad?" Her eyes blaze. "Why do you always have to get so angry? Do you know how embarrassing it is when the whole street hears you fighting?"

Dad, whose face was already red, is now turning almost purple.

"We were having a discussion, sweetheart. Adults do that sometimes."

"So when me and Elias argue, it's not OK, but when you and Mom do it, it is OK?"

"Sweetie, please, I…"

Zaid leans forward.

"So, you were fighting. And then you followed her."

He looks at Elias and then at Alice. There is pity on his face. "I think we'd better continue this conversation down at the station, without the children."

Dad's face hardens.

"Am I suspected of something?"

"We just want to be able to talk undisturbed. Do you have any relatives or neighbors who can look after the kids for a while?"

Elias sees Dad's jaw muscles tense, as if he would much rather tell the cops to get lost, but he restrains himself and responds almost calmly.

"My mother lives in Malmö, and besides she's too old. My brother lives in Spain. Tien's family is in Vietnam, and we've never met them, truth be told. As for the neighbors…" Dad glances at the Ingemarssons' house across the street. "Well, we don't know each other all that well."

Frida gets up, brings her phone to her ear, and takes a few steps out into the hall. "I'm calling social."

Dad gets up. His voice falters.

"What do you mean you're calling social?"

"I'm afraid it's necessary," says Frida. "The kids have to be taken into protective custody while we work this out."

She disappears out of sight. Elias hears her talking heatedly to someone.

Everything is happening so fast. Much too fast. Are the police going to take Dad away? With Mom already gone? Elias wants to say something, to shout and scream and stop them, but no sound comes out. His fingers clasp his tablet so hard his knuckles go white. The cartoon has finished without him noticing. He looks up at Alice but her eyes are fixed on Dad.

Zaid stands up.

"And I'm going to need the keys to the Mazda," he says.

"Why?" Dad asks.

"It's just a routine check. We always do it in cases like this."

Dad takes his bunch of keys from his pocket, removes the car key and tosses it to him.

"Here."

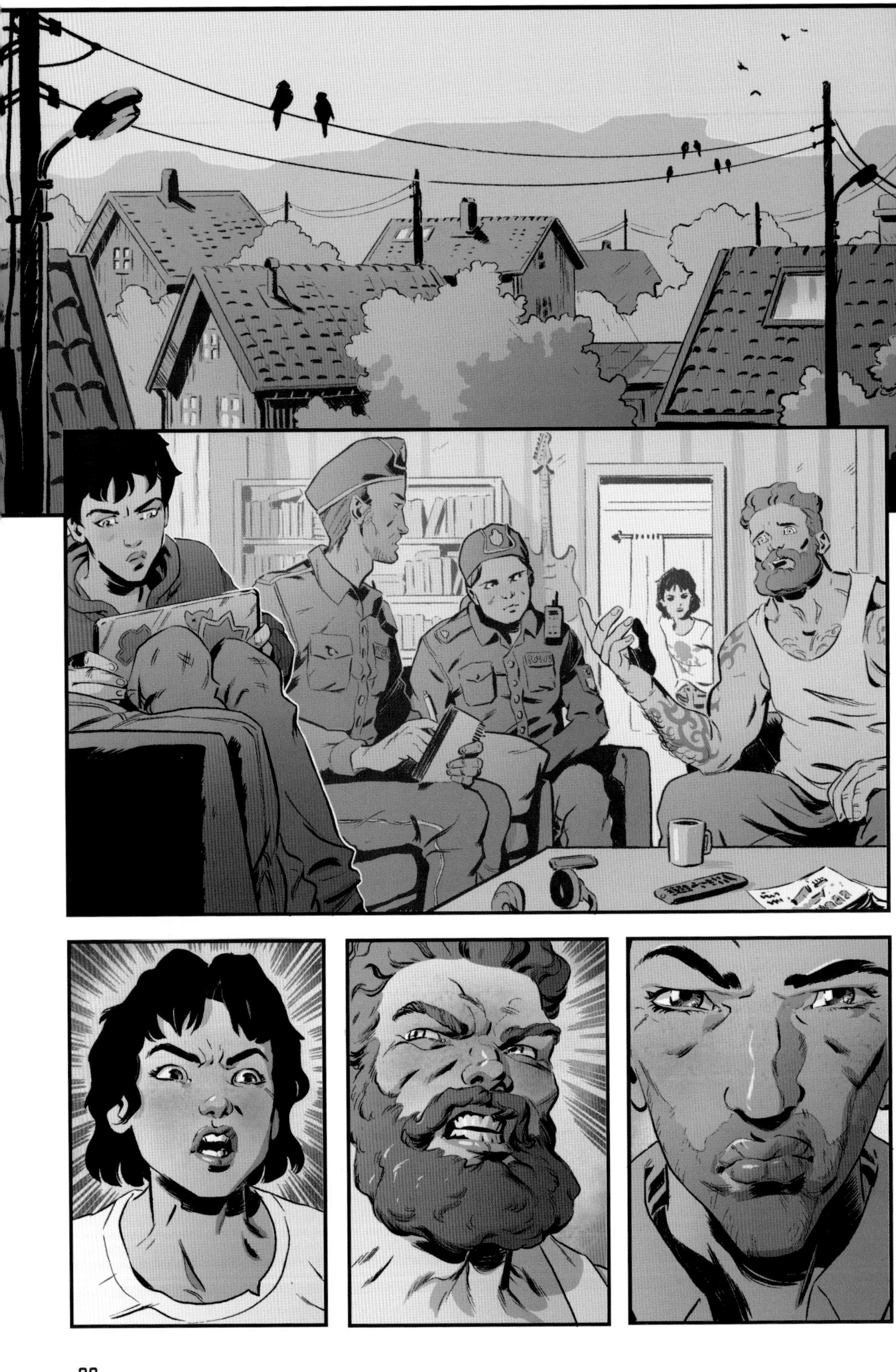

"Thanks."

Zaid disappears out the front door just as Frida returns.

"Here's what's going to happen now," she says. "You're going to accompany my colleague down to the station for further questioning. I'll wait here with the children until social services arrive. They'll have to spend the night in one of our emergency shelters."

Alice gives a start and takes a step backwards.

"We're not going anywhere!" she says firmly. "We can take care of ourselves. We're not little kids. And what if…" She swallows and clears her throat. Elias can see she is close to tears. "What if Mom comes back? Someone should be here."

For a moment Frida looks almost sad. Then it occurs to Elias that she knows something she's not letting on. She soon collects herself.

"I'm afraid that's not for you to decide," she tells Alice. "You have to go."

"I don't want to!"

Zaid comes back through the front door.

"There are blood stains in the back trunk of the Mazda," he says. "Whose blood is it?"

"It's Tien's," says Dad. "We went to the recycling center this week and she cut herself on a can."

Zaid steps purposefully into the living room, followed by the two police officers from the other car.

"I'm truly sorry. I really didn't want to have to do this in front of your kids. But I'm afraid you're going to have to come with us. I'm arresting you on suspicion of involvement in the disappearance of Tien Johansson."

ELIAS

Dad has been arrested! Elias can hardly believe it. This can't be happening! What do the police know that they're not saying? Could Dad actually have done something? It's such an awful thought that he immediately tries to dismiss it, but it stays with him, gnawing away inside.

"Are you crazy?" Dad's voice booms. "I called you to help me find my wife. And now you think I've done something?"

"According to your neighbors, you were gone for nearly two hours. And there's blood in the car. Surely you can see that something seems off." Zaid pulls out a pair of handcuffs. "Come quietly now. If you're innocent you have nothing to worry about. We'll sort it all out."

Frida turns to Elias and Alice.

"Come on. Let's go into the kitchen for a minute."

"No!" says Alice.

Elias would love to go into the kitchen. And then up the stairs and into his room so he can close the door, crawl into bed, and never leave.

"But she's out there somewhere!" Dad shouts. "You're

wasting time! You have to listen to me."

"Please, just come quietly," says Zaid.

"Are those really necessary?" Dad glares at the handcuffs.

"They are for your safety, and ours. We don't want anyone getting hurt."

"But this is ridiculous! I…"

Alice jumps to her feet and stands in between Dad and the police.

"Leave him alone! Mom and Dad argue sometimes but they love each other! Dad would never hurt her!"

"I'm really sorry," says Zaid. "He has to come with us. But there's no need to worry. We're just going to ask him a few questions. I'm sure everything will be fine and he'll be back home soon."

"No!" screams Alice. Her shrill voice hurts Elias' ears. "You can't take him!"

Dad bends down, puts his arms around Alice and kisses her hair. Then he gently pushes her aside.

"That's enough now, sweetheart. I'll be back before you know it. I promise, I…"

Dad's voice breaks and his huge body deflates but he manages to stay upright. Elias has never seen him like this.

"Let's get this over with," he says.

The police handcuff Dad and lead him out through the front door. Elias stares at them.

"Karin from social services is on her way," says Frida.

"She's going to take you to the emergency shelter. You can talk to the staff there if you want." She looks at Elias and Alice in turn and clears her throat as if trying to find the words.

"Are you OK?" she eventually squeezes out.

Elias can't answer. The knot in his stomach is too big, swallowing up his words, suffocating his thoughts.

"How the hell do you think we are?!" Alice snaps, turning on her heel and stomping off into the kitchen.

Frida sighs and sinks down into the armchair. She looks tired and rubs her face.

"Christ, what a day," she mutters to herself.

Elias hears the fridge door open in the kitchen. Then Alice starts clattering around with the crockery.

"I'm just going to make a sandwich," she says.

Frida nods, picks up her phone and starts reading something.

Elias has barely stepped into the kitchen before Alice grabs hold of him. She pulls him over to the sink and turns the tap on full blast.

"So she can't hear us..." she whispers, nodding towards the living room. "I saw it in a spy movie once."

"They took Dad." Elias wants to say more, but the words won't come out.

"Yeah. Idiots. They don't know Dad. He would never ever hurt Mom."

She is utterly convinced. Elias can't be so sure. Dad did follow her. And that thing about the blood. Elias doesn't remember anything about Mom cutting herself on a can. But then again Mom had always been a quick healer. And she's not one to complain. She always says that people in Vietnam don't go to the doctor unless they've broken a bone.

"But what if something happened?" he says tentatively.

Alice doesn't listen.

"The police are going to drive us to some home where we'll sit and waste away." She crosses her arms. "I won't go! Mom might have gotten hurt in Lunsen! She might have had a fall or something!"

Images of his mother's lifeless body flash through his mind. Lying in a ditch or under a fallen tree.

"Nobody is out there looking for her!" Alice continues. "That means we have to do it ourselves."

"What are you saying?"

"Let's go. Now. Before that policewoman suspects anything."

Elias peeks into the living room. Alice is right. They have to find Mom.

Water is still gushing from the tap as they hurry over to the back door that opens out into the garden. On the wall by the door hang Mom's and Alice's fencing equipment: thin sheath-swords, buckler shields and parrying daggers. Below them, two pairs of sneakers are waiting neatly. Alice quickly puts hers on and signals for Elias to do the same. Then she opens the door as quietly as she can and they are greeted by the warm evening air. It smells like flowers and Elias sees humming bumblebees on their last outing of the day among the apple trees and rose bushes.

Carefully, they sneak over the grass, past the garden furniture with its peeling white paint, and over to the garage. They find their bikes.

It suddenly dawns on Elias that they are about to run away from the police.

"What if they get angry?" he whispers. "Will they put us in prison?"

"Don't be silly!" Alice snaps. "Children can't go to jail."

Then they hear a shout from inside the house.

"Hello? Where are you?"

Through the open patio door, Elias can see Frida move quickly through the kitchen. Then she glances through the window and sees them. He meets her gaze. They stand there for a full second before Alice jumps onto her bike.

"Come on!"

"No," Frida screams. "Stop right there!"

But Elias is already on his bike. He pedals for dear

life, behind Alice, street after street through the Sunnersta neighborhood. Clouds move across the sky.

To the north the evening sky glows from the city lights. Alice veers off towards the water, whizzes across Flottsund Bridge and on towards Lunsen, the vast dark forest.

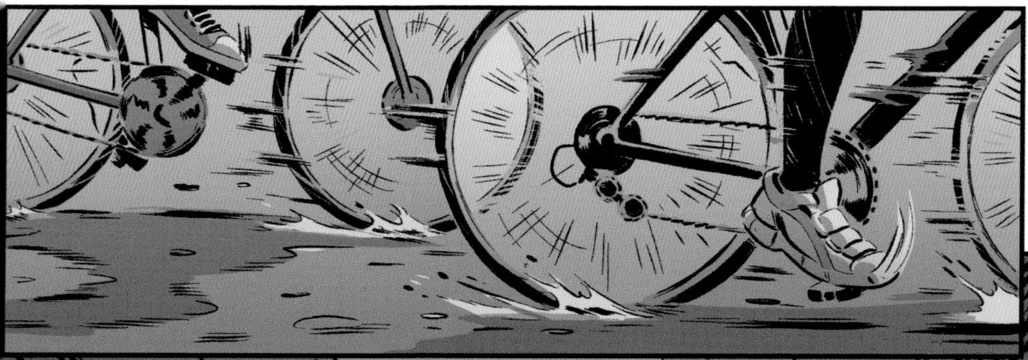
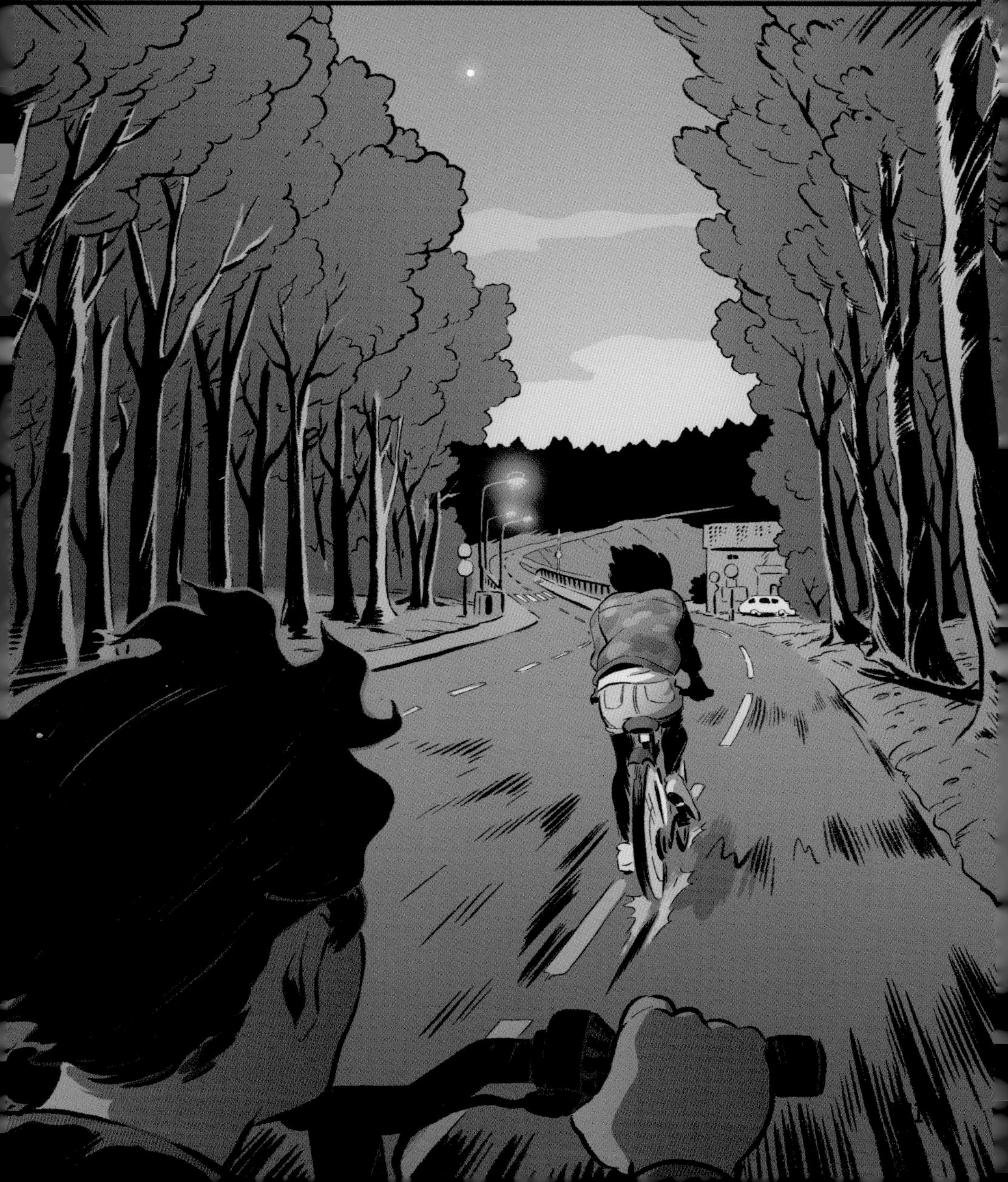

ALICE

Alice walks her bike onto the path and Elias is right behind her. She can hear his rapid, shallow breathing.

"We park here," she says, picking up her bike and throwing it into a bush.

She doesn't bother locking it up. It doesn't matter any more. Elias, on the other hand, locks his bike carefully and places the key in his pocket.

The path leads straight into the pitch black woods. Alice peers into the darkness, willing it to reveal all its secrets.

"Mom always goes to that tree up on the rocks," she says. "I've gone with her a bunch of times and helped set up sensors and measuring equipment. I'd know my way there blindfolded in the middle of the night."

"It is the middle of the night," Elias says, shivering.

"Yeah, yeah, you know what I mean."

A cold wind blows through the trees, but Alice feels strengthened by the cold.

"That policewoman," Elias continues. "Frida. She knew something. When you said we should wait for Mom, in case she came home again, she looked…"

"That doesn't necessarily mean anything."

"No, of course not…" he chokes.

She can see that Elias is upset. Suddenly all she wants to do is take him in her arms and hold him until this nightmare is over. But she can't. They have a mission. If there's even the slightest chance that Mom is out there somewhere, they have to find her.

They walk silently along the path. Alice takes out her phone and turns on the flashlight. The battery won't last long, but it's something at least… And when it dies, they'll just have to manage without it.

They walk past ponds and swamps. Moonlight glitters on the water. Veils of fog move between the trees and there's an odd, intermittent rustling in the bushes, as if some large creature is moving around in there. Probably just a deer, Alice tells herself.

She can't believe the police arrested Dad! They put handcuffs on him and took him away. Anger boils up inside her again. What complete and utter idiots! They have no idea!

All the same, she probably shouldn't have barked at Dad in front of the police like that. But he was being so dense! Didn't he realize they would figure out that he and mom had been arguing? Dad is an idiot too. Still, all she wants to do right now is hug him. She wishes she hadn't refused his hug in the garage. She can still feel the spot on her head where he kissed her, before he was taken away.

Where is he now? In an interrogation room somewhere? Like in the movies, with him sitting at a table opposite of angry, questioning police officers? Dad would only give angry answers, which wouldn't go too well…

She groans. Earlier today, her biggest concern was passing her math test. Now it feels so insignificant and far away.

Elias suddenly starts to sing. He's odd like that; he just does whatever he feels like. But the lyrics slowly dawn on her and a lump forms in her throat.

The Phoenix travels through space at night
With five horns on its head
Sleep my two and enjoy her journey
Let the dream come true
Seven came
Two came
Four sheep came
Let's count them
Three came
Five came
Eight sheep came
Manna rains from heaven

No one can see the future
Keep the song inside you
No, no one can see the future
Keep the song inside you

It's a lullaby that Mom used to sing when they were very little. Elias stops singing, but Alice can still hear the words, and her mother's deep singing voice. It makes her feel safe. Tears run down her cheeks and she hastily wipes them away. She has to be strong now, for herself and for Elias. He can't see her break down. She grits her teeth and picks up the pace.

Half an hour later, they arrive.

"There it is," Alice says, pointing.

A cliff protrudes from the forest and a lonely, ancient tree balances on the crest. Alice quickly climbs up the rocks and Elias follows. When she gets to the tree she reaches into the branches and takes out a plastic box, no bigger than a hockey puck.

"Here's the sensor." She inspects it closely using the light on her phone. "I think she put this one here yesterday."

"How do you know?"

"Because it isn't covered in pollen yet. The plastic attracts pollen like crazy. In another two days it would be completely yellow."

"So she was here?"

Alice looks around, again trying to force the darkness to reveal its secrets.

"She was here. Come on, let's look for footprints."

The ground is grey and unfamiliar in the faint phone light. She doesn't say they should look for a body, but that's all she can think of as they walk around the rocky cliff, searching through thickets and bushes. Mom could be here somewhere, hurt, unconscious, or worse...

They search without success and come back to the tree. Alice holds her hands to her mouth and shouts as loud as she can.

"Mooooom! Mooooom!"

The sound disappears into the forest, swallowed by the night. Deathly silence returns.

"Let's shout together," says Elias.

He puts his hands to his mouth and yells as loud as he can. They stand there shouting together for a long time. But nothing happens. No one comes.

Then Elias breaks down and the tears flow down his face. It hurts Alice to see him like that. She has to try again. She screams until her voice is hoarse and her throat is sore. They both stand there silently on the cliff, brother, and sister, alone in the darkness.

Then something moves in the forest. Alice squints to see better. Is it an animal? Elias sees it too and gasps. At

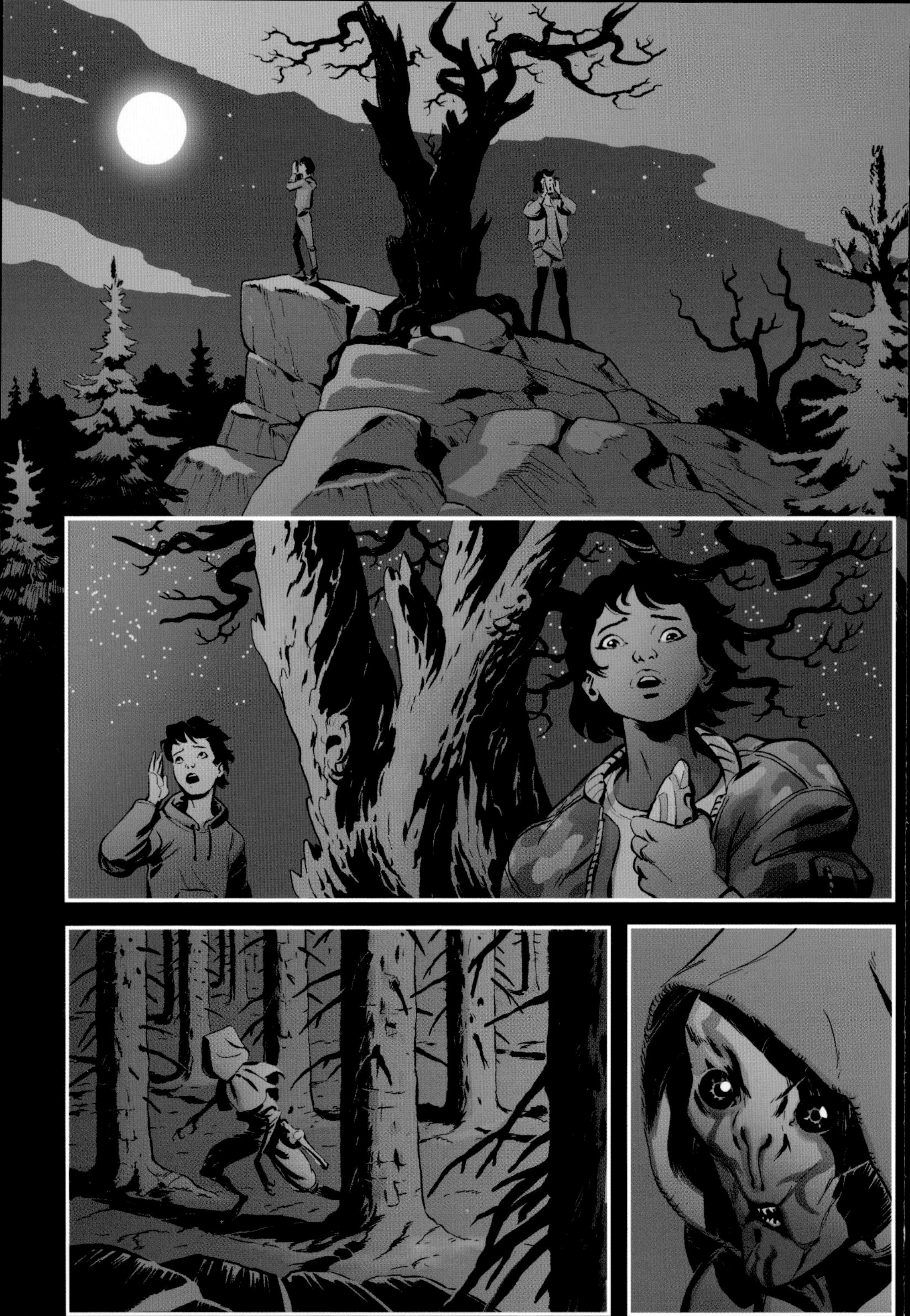

first she thinks it's a man dressed in black coming towards them through the blueberry bushes; but there's something not quite right about it. Whatever it is, its movements aren't human, they are fast and lurching. With its long black robe and belt around the waist, it looks like a mixture between a monk and ninja.

It stops at the bottom of the cliff and looks up at them, its eyes big and shiny. Much larger than human eyes. They are completely black, like a bottomless lake. Alice feels nausea rise up in her stomach. She's never seen anything like it; she suspects no one has.

As if possessed, Alice's right hand moves to take out her phone, open the camera and flash a shaft of light straight onto the creature's face. It shrieks and turns its head away. In the photo, Alice sees that its skin is bluish-purple with green streaks. It has a mouth, but only narrow notches where the nose should be.

The creature rubs its eyes and pulls a long, curved knife from its belt.

"Grus ta prok," it says. Its voice is creaky and not in the least bit human.

Alice doesn't dare move. She hardly dares breathe. Her heart is pounding.

"Grus ta prok," the creature says again, pointing at mom's plastic box.

Its hand only has four fingers.

Alice doesn't answer. She tightens her grip on the box. The creature growls, raises the knife, and attacks.

ALICE

Alice can hardly believe her eyes. The creature, whatever it is, races towards them up the cliff. A long dagger gleams in its hand. Panic sweeps over Alice and she casts a quick glance at Elias who's standing next to her unmoving. She grabs him by the arm and pulls him away. She drops her phone in the confusion and doesn't dare pick it up.

"Run!"

Together they rush down the other side of the cliff.

Elias jolts back to life and picks up the pace. He's a fast runner. One of the fastest at school. But Alice is faster, with longer legs and more stamina. She glances back now and then to make sure he doesn't fall behind. What on earth was that thing? Was that what took Mom? And why does it want the sensor? She vows she'll never let them have it. She grips the plastic box so hard her hand shakes.

They come across a new trail and move deeper into the forest. It's hard to see in the dark, but Alice knows the terrain well, having spent a lot of time out here with her science youth group. She knows every inch, every lake and pond.

Surely the same can't be said of the thing chasing them? It still feels like the creature is close. Now and then she hears a stumble or a splash. Maybe its night vision isn't too good? Or it's still blinded after the flash from her camera?

"Grus ta prok, ekivit selmani kro!" It yells at them.

She has no idea what it's saying and has no intention of asking.

They dash over stone slabs and run through paths and thickets. Alice feels her muscles giving away. Elias stumbles in front of her. He's starting to lose momentum too. He won't last much longer.

They reach a barbecue area where they sometimes picnic and cook sausages in the summer. There is an observation tower, a few lean-to shelters, and a brick fireplace. Running at full speed through the rest area, they jump over one of the benches and disappear into the forest. They hear a bang and a series of hisses behind them.

Just when they've got a good lead, Elias stumbles on a tree root and nearly falls face first into a blueberry bush. At the last second, he manages to catch his footing and stay upright.

She realizes they have to chance it.

"In here," she says, tugging Elias down behind a shrub. "Whatever happens, you have to stay right here! And take this." She pushes the plastic box into his hands. "Don't make a sound."

CHAPTER 8

The creature has started moving again. Alice hears its rapid footsteps getting closer and closer. Without waiting for an answer from Elias, she sets off along the path and runs with all her might. She can hear the monster and it's following her.

Now she can really speed up. She runs for her life. But the creature's eyes must have grown accustomed to the darkness because it doesn't seem to be stumbling as much as before. She glances over her shoulder and sees the grotesque figure charging towards her with a sharp blade flashing in its hand. Terror floods her body, but she doesn't let it paralyze her. Instead she uses it to run faster. She moves effortlessly, practically flying. The ground rushes past and the trees become a black blur.

Suddenly, something heavy strikes her from behind. She crashes to the ground, tumbles over and lands on her back. In two seconds, the creature is on top of her. Its neck is craned far back as it raises its dagger.

"Prok, prok, messeria to doh!"

Its black eyes are terrifying. When it speaks, its narrow nostrils, or whatever they are, vibrate and its mouth opens to reveal sharp, shiny teeth.

Alice screams. A scream of pure terror. It cuts through the forest and echoes between the trees.

The creature gives her a cryptic stare, then stabs the dagger into her left shoulder.

Pain explodes through her arm and up into her skull. Alice screams again. All her energy drains away. Something hot and sticky seeps through her clothes. Then come the tears.

"Grus doh! Grus doh!" the creature shouts.

Is this the end? Is she going to die now? White flashes of pain slash through her body. There is a whistling roar in her ears and she can barely breathe.

"I don't understand," she squeezes out. "Please. Let me go."

The creature pulls the dagger out of her shoulder and blood pours from the wound. Then it moves the blade a few inches, bringing the sharp edge to her throat.

"Selmon drocht."

"Please…"

ALICE

The creature slowly drags the tip of the knife along Alice's neck, grazing her skin. Just a little more pressure and she will be done for. Pain blazes through her shoulder and her sweater becomes warm and wet with blood. Her blood.

She can't make out any emotion on the creature's face, just an icy ruthlessness.

"Selmon drocht ta."

But she can't respond. Can't beg for mercy. The words die in her throat. She can think them, but can't say them out loud. Please stop. I want to live. Please, please...

A black shadow emerges from the forest. She can't see what it is through her tears and the darkness around her, but it's the size of a bear, or even bigger. It smashes into the creature above her with enough force to send it flying several feet. The creature slams down and the shadowy figure jumps and pins it to the ground.

Alice presses her hand to the wound on her shoulder and tries to get up, but her whole body is shaking. She doesn't have the strength to sit up on the damp grass. Her shoulder throbs and she falls back down, powerless. She struggles to breathe between sobs, blood flowing through her fingers.

The creature is kicking and stabbing wildly, but its opponent is much larger, in fact, in an entirely different weight class. After a minute of struggle, the creature manages to get loose and jumps headlong into the trees, vanishing in a flash.

The looming shadow gets up and walks over to her. She tries to focus on her rescuer, but big white spots dance in her eyes. She blinks. As she wipes her tears with one hand, her vision clears. But she is met with an entirely unbelievable sight. Bending over her is a lizard-like figure. He has a wide mouth with sharp teeth, a crown of horns on its head, and shimmering, reptilian eyes. His skin is covered in tough armor-like scales. And he's wearing some sort of red uniform, a coat cut and sewn for a creature significantly larger than a human. The hilt to a huge sword hangs over one shoulder. Around his waist is a belt with storage pockets, knives hanging from the sides, and what look to be firearms.

The reptile kneels down, notices that Alice is bleeding and grunts something.

"I don't understand you," she whispers.

A short beep comes from a small receiver on his forearm. Then she hears a woman's voice, speaking in a lilting accent.

"Brock is asking if you're OK."

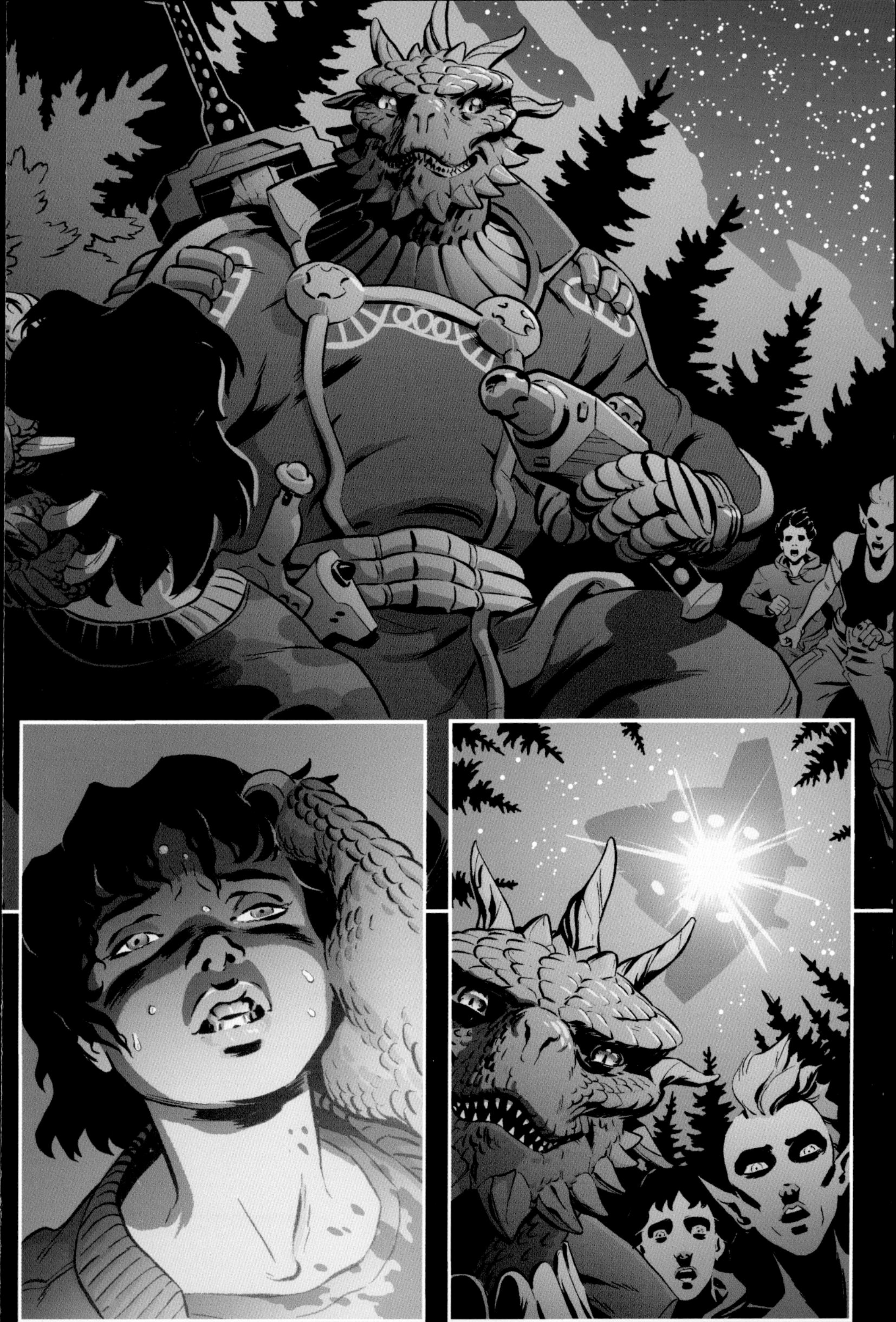

"If I'm OK?" Alice almost laughs, which makes her shoulder hurt again. "I'm lying here bleeding."

"So close the wound."

"What do you mean, close?"

This is too much. She feels herself begin to space out. This is just a dream, a totally absurd dream. Mom isn't missing. Dad hasn't been arrested. Elias isn't sitting alone somewhere shivering in the woods. She hasn't been stabbed and definitely isn't bleeding while talking to a receiver attached to the forearm of a uniformed dinosaur.

"The wound," the receiver says again. "Can you close it?"

"What are you talking about?"

The receiver begins to hiss and click. It must be speaking the lizard's language because the giant figure opens his eyes wide in realization, pulls a small gun from his belt, brings it to Alice's shoulder and pulls the trigger. She braces herself for a bang, too tired to even consider escape, but no shot is fired. Instead, a sticky grey liquid flows from the barrel and down into the wound. It's almost like a glue gun. The sticky substance is warm and feels good on her skin. Her shoulder suddenly hurts less, almost as if the grey goo is absorbing the pain. Soon it solidifies and the wound stops bleeding.

There is a rustle in the bushes. It's Elias limping towards her! Her sweet, beloved little brother. He made it. A tall woman is walking beside him. Finally, an adult in all this madness.

CHAPTER 9

Elias throws himself down onto the grass, flings his arms around her, and hugs her hard.

"Are you OK? Tell me you're OK," he gasps. "They found me. I told them you were in danger. But I didn't know where you were."

She hugs him back with all the strength she has left in her body, which isn't much. Sleep is slowing her down, staying awake seems impossible. She wonders if this is how it feels to go into shock. Nothing feels real anymore.

Her vision is blurry but she tries to focus on the woman who arrived with Elias. Maybe she can help them get home. Talk to the police. But there is something strange about her. She has a really cool punk looking hairstyle, with the red hair sticking straight up, but there's something weird about her face. First, Alice thinks it's just the darkness playing tricks on her, but then she realizes that the woman's complexion is blue. And her eyes are strangely orange.

When Alice sees the woman's ears, she starts giggling. They're pointy like elf ears! It's just all so bizarre. Laughter bubbles from her chest.

A dark shadow glides over the treetops. It looks like an airplane, but with a round shape and small wings. It's flying in perfect silence. Six lights shine in a circle on its underside. The craft stops directly above them, and the lizard looks up and hisses.

Then a huge spotlight shines down from the sky. It bathes her in light. She feels her body being pulled upwards. Slowly she is lifted from the ground, floating between the trees, towards the sky. The light is warm. It envelops her and comforts her. She lets it take her.

After all, this is only a dream.

BROCK

Brock steps into the light and lets the shuttle's tractor beam lift him off the ground. Blood flows from a deep stab wound in his side. The Krao are lethal warriors, much stronger than their long, slender figures would suggest. Brock concentrates on healing and the wound stops bleeding.

The girl he rescued is floating above him. She seems to have lost consciousness. If he had arrived a few seconds later she could have died. Have these Krao no honor? He knows that they hate the Alonai, but to attack children! Parishvi's children!

Where is Parishvi anyway? Were they too late? Has she already been taken prisoner by the Krao? A dull growl rises from Brock's chest. If the Krao have hurt her, they will regret it bitterly. He will hunt them until his dying day.

He looks down. Syndra has taken a firm hold of the boy and stepped into the beam. She really should have waited a few more menes. But Syndra doesn't like waiting. Brock flicks the tip of his tail in resignation. He's going to have to step into the shuttle quickly, otherwise she will bash into him with her hard head. Again. She is always in a hurry and her skull is surprisingly tough. For an Alonai, that is.

Brock rises through the hatch of the shuttle and turns his body for a smooth landing on the cargo compartment floor. The girl's body is floating near the ceiling, directly beneath the tractor beam generator. He pulls her out of the beam and catches her body gently in his arms. Then he hurries to pull his tail out of the way before Syndra and the boy come through.

He looks at the girl's face. These are Parishvi's children. Arisa was sure of it and Brock knows better than to question her when it comes to such things. She can carry out detailed facial analysis and recognize familial relations in a thousandth of a mene. Personally, Brock thinks most Alonai look the same, except Syndra. He would recognize her angry eyes anywhere. He chuckles to himself.

Just then, Syndra arrives with the boy.

"What are you laughing at?" she asks.

"Nothing."

Brock gently lays the girl down on the floor. At the same time, the boy frees himself from Syndra, runs straight to his sister and tries to talk to her. She is unconscious. Brock doesn't understand a word he's saying.

"What language are they speaking?"

"It's called Swedish," says Arisa from the roof. "A regional language with only a few million speakers. I'll analyze it and add it to the nanites' database. You should be able to talk to them soon."

The tractor beam switches off and the hatch closes.

"It would be good if we could catch that Krao," says Syndra. "They might have important information."

"Arisa. Can you locate the Krao?" Brock asks.

"I'm afraid not," says Arisa. "The shuttle sensors are finding no traces of them."

The scales on Brock's chest contract and his tail drums on the floor a couple of times. His side itches where the wound is closing up.

Brock looks at the children. They are so pale. Completely the wrong skin color for Alonai. And there is something off with their ears, too.

The boy turns to him and says something, quick and pleading. Tears are flowing down his cheeks. The girl is still lying behind him, seemingly lifeless. She needs help. Now!

"To the Phoenix!" Brock growls. "Arisa, prepare the sickbay! We have no time to lose."

The weak whir of the engines heighten into a roar and the shuttle speeds up and away from the planet known as Earth.

ALICE

The first thing Alice notices when she wakes up is the smell. Or rather, the lack of smell. It doesn't smell like her bedroom at home, sun-warmed and slightly humid. It doesn't smell damp and lush like the forest. The air is dry and clinical, like a hospital.

She hates hospitals.

She opens her eyes slowly. The room is bright and the walls are metal but painted in shades of muted blue. There are strange machines with hoses and tubes, kind of similar to ones in hospital TV shows, but different somehow.

Something clings to her head with lots of little metal plates pressed against her scalp. It rattles when she shakes her head. The plates are released and pulled upwards by a bundle of tentacles that disappears into an opening in the ceiling.

She opens her eyes wide with a shudder. Then she realizes someone is sleeping in a chair next to her. It's Elias! She tries to speak but it comes out as little more than a hoarse hiss. Her little brother wakes up anyway.

"Alice!"

He jumps to his feet and throws his arms around her. She has a foggy memory of him doing the same thing very recently.

"Water," she rasps.

"Of course." He takes a quick look around. "Wait!"

He rushes to a little hatch in the wall and says in a loud voice:

"A glass of water please."

A soft woman's voice comes from the ceiling.

"Here you are."

There is a whirring sound and Elias takes a cup from the hatch. He brings it to Alice's lips and she drinks greedily. The water is perfect, just the right temperature.

She clears her throat.

"Who was that?" Her voice is still shaky but she can just about speak.

"Who was what?" says Elias.

"The woman's voice."

"It's not a woman. It's Arisa. Oh, I have so much to tell you!" He starts jumping up and down in excitement. "We're not on Earth anymore. We're on a spaceship."

Some water goes down the wrong way and Alice starts to cough. A spaceship?

Memories suddenly flash through her mind. There is a flurry of images and she presses one hand to her temple. It all comes flooding back to her like a mighty gushing river.

CHAPTER 11

Running like mad through Lunsen. Being chased by a strange creature with black, inhuman eyes and narrow notches for nostrils. It had a knife and stabbed her in the shoulder! And then there was a lizard and a blue elf with pointy ears.

The headache goes away as quickly as it came. She starts laughing. A lizard and an elf. That's impossible, isn't it? She reaches for her shoulder. It doesn't hurt. No bandage, no wounds, nothing. Her skin is healthy and strong with no trace of a scar.

"It was just a dream," she says to herself.

"It's not a dream," says Elias, almost insulted. "We're on a spaceship!"

"Oh stop," she snaps. "What hospital are we at? What really happened?"

Elias looks up at the ceiling.

"Arisa," he says loudly and clearly. "Where are we?"

"You are on a spaceship called In the Eye of the Storm Rises the Phoenix, but it is commonly referred to simply as the Phoenix."

Alice sits up carefully, propping herself up on both arms, and looks around. On closer inspection this infirmary looks very different from a typical hospital.

"Arisa?" she says tentatively.

"Yes."

"Who are you?"

The answer comes immediately.

"I am what you would call an artificial intelligence, or synthetic person. My program runs on the Phoenix's central computer and I am responsible for maintaining the various systems of the ship and for helping the crew with their work."

"So you're a kind of robot?"

Arisa laughs. The sound ripples through the room. It sounds so genuine.

"Not really. I don't have a body like robots do. I don't walk around the ship's corridors. But if it makes it easier for you to think of me as a robot, please feel free to do so. In which case, you might say that the whole ship is my body, and I am like a huge sea creature, but instead of swimming in the ocean I swim through a sea of stars."

"See?" says Elias. "Arisa. Show her what's outside."

A huge screen pops up. It hovers in mid-air above the bed. At first the screen is dark, but then it shows Earth. Her home planet is floating in space, blue and green and white. Like a shiny jewel in the middle of all the darkness.

This is impossible! But she can see Earth right there. She reaches forward to touch the screen. Her hand moves straight through it.

"It's just a hologram," says Arisa. "But it shows an accurate picture of what your planet looks like from the ship. We are currently in orbit around the Earth, about 100,000 miles from its surface."

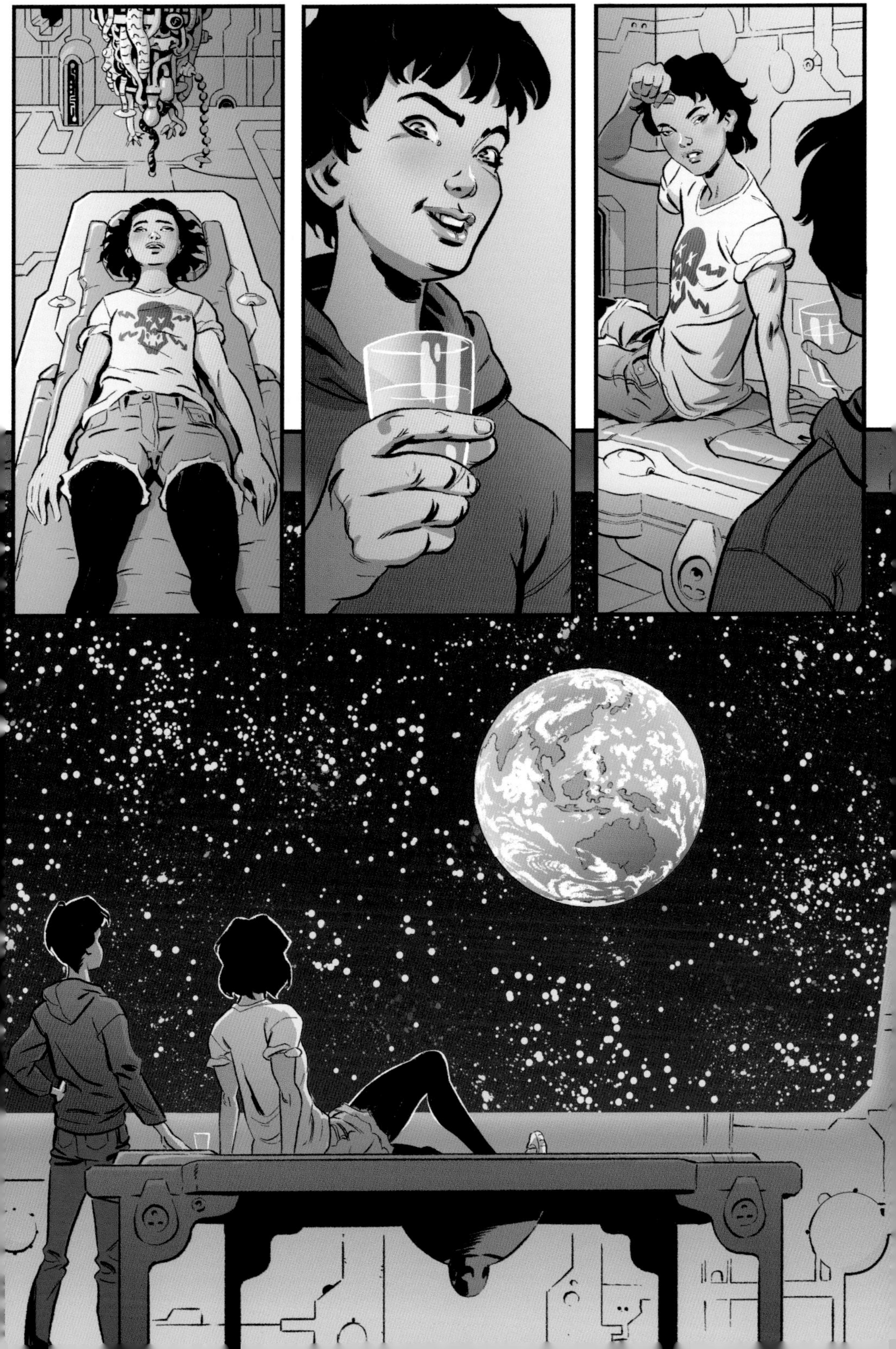

There's a faint buzzing sound and the doors to what Alice is beginning to believe might indeed be a ship's sickbay, slide open and disappear into the wall. In the doorway stands the giant lizard from the forest.

ALICE

Alice's head is spinning. Her last hope that this was all nothing but a weird dream has just been shattered. It really is true. They really are in space and these inhuman creatures do exist. This also means that Mom has disappeared and Dad has been arrested. And that the monster with the knife… She shakes her head and focuses on the visitor.

The lizard is dressed in the same red uniform as before. The colors perfectly complement his large green scales. The horns on his head look like a crown and he has several smaller horns protruding from his cheeks and chin.

His appearance is terrifying, but he looks at her with what she supposes is a smile, and she sees kindness in the yellow eyes. He opens his mouth, exposing rows of powerful, sharp teeth, and strange noises come out. Hums, hisses, and clicks.

"Welcome aboard. I hope you feel better."

Alice gives a start.

It's not Swedish. It's not any human language. And yet…

"I understand you…"

"Good," says the lizard. "It makes everything a lot easier

when we can talk to each other. I'm the captain of this ship and my name is…" He makes a throaty cluck and a slurping sound. But Alice clearly hears: "Brock Stregga."

"Nice to meet you, Brock," she says automatically.

The lizard looks pleased.

"Nice to meet you too, Alice."

His attempt to pronounce 'Alice' ends in a long, lispy sssss. Still, she understands him perfectly.

"But how…?"

"We've activated your nanites," says Arisa from the ceiling. "For some reason they were turned off. If we hadn't started them up you could have died. It was close. You lost a lot of blood."

"What? What are nanites? "

"Microscopic robots. They are so small that they're invisible to the naked eye. They exist throughout your body. As a second immune system. In addition to healing your wounds, they help you understand all languages spoken by the civilized races of the old empire's enclaves."

Alice holds her head in her hands. This is too much information to take in at once.

"Are you strong enough to take a walk?" asks Brock.

"I think so."

"Come then."

Alice drags her feet as they walk through the ship's corridors on their way to… she doesn't know where they're going. She is so very tired. Elias yawns loudly next to her but then looks up at her and grins from ear to ear. Despite everything that has happened, despite Mom's disappearance, he is clearly ecstatic to be on a spaceship. His nerdy brain cells are probably having a dance party, and she has no intention of taking that joy away from him.

Her thoughts are preoccupied with what Brock wants to show them. Why did he and that blue woman show up in the woods? Why did they bring her and Elias to the ship? Not that she's ungrateful – after all, she was lying on the ground bleeding and they saved her. But what do they want? Do they know anything about Mom?

So many questions.

"How long was I unconscious?"

Elias takes out his phone. She sees that it has no reception. Obviously. The time is 3:00 a.m. It's the middle of the night.

"Maybe four hours."

Within the space of four hours she has been rescued from a monster in Lunsen, flown out into space, and her shoulder has not only been tended to, but completely healed by some kind of microscopic machines in her body. The same microscopic machines that are also allowing her to understand what a bunch of aliens are saying. In four hours!

They arrive at a door that opens automatically in front of them and Brock gestures for them to enter.

"Welcome to the bridge. This is the ship's mission control

center. From here we steer the ship, navigate the stars and even fire our weapon systems if we encounter an enemy. My crew is not here right now but you will meet them soon."

Alice steps in through the door with Elias close behind. She looks around. The room is shaped like a semicircle with a huge hologram screen on the far wall. On it is the same image of Earth as she saw from sickbay.

A row of screens and strange controls runs along the curved walls. Directly in front of her is a giant armchair with a large hole between the seat cushion and the backrest. Alice leans back discreetly to take a peek at Brock's back. Of course he has a tail. A long, green, scaly tail with sharp spikes on the outside of the tip. In front of the armchair is a control panel with gently glowing buttons. Small screens and holographic symbols dance in the air above.

"Is that your chair?" Elias says, pointing to the armchair.

"That's right," says Brock. "I've spent a lot of time in it."

To the left of Brock's armchair is something more human sized, like a car seat, also with a control panel in front of it. Compared to everything else on the ship it looks almost normal, like something from home. From Earth. Alice shakes her head. She isn't on Earth anymore. Her brain still can't get used to the idea.

To the right is another control panel. But this one has no chair. Instead, there is a tree branch attached to the floor.

Alice thinks she can even see bark on it. What kind of creature sits there?

"Oh boy, this is so cool!" Elias exclaims. He runs up to one of the hologram screens on the wall and looks at the diagram on it. "This is our solar system, huh?"

Alice studies the symbols. Elias is right. She recognizes the planets: Mercury, Venus, Earth, Mars, Jupiter, Saturn – the one with the rings – Uranus and Neptune. Mom used to talk about them sometimes when they were out walking in Lunsen. And about stars. Mom always liked astronomy. Alice feels a stab in her heart. Suddenly she misses her mother so much it hurts. If only they could find her now, she would tell her how much she loves her, let out all those words that are usually so difficult to say.

The doors slide open behind them. The woman from the forest comes in. She is dressed in baggy purple trousers and a black and bright red top to match her equally bright red hair. But it's not the clothes Alice is staring at. In this bright light there is no doubt: she really does have blue skin, golden-orange eyes and pointed ears.

"This is Syndra Faetor, my second in command," says Brock.

"You look better," says Syndra, running her hand through her hair.

Alice is horrified to realize that her entire left arm is made of metal. Syndra nods to her.

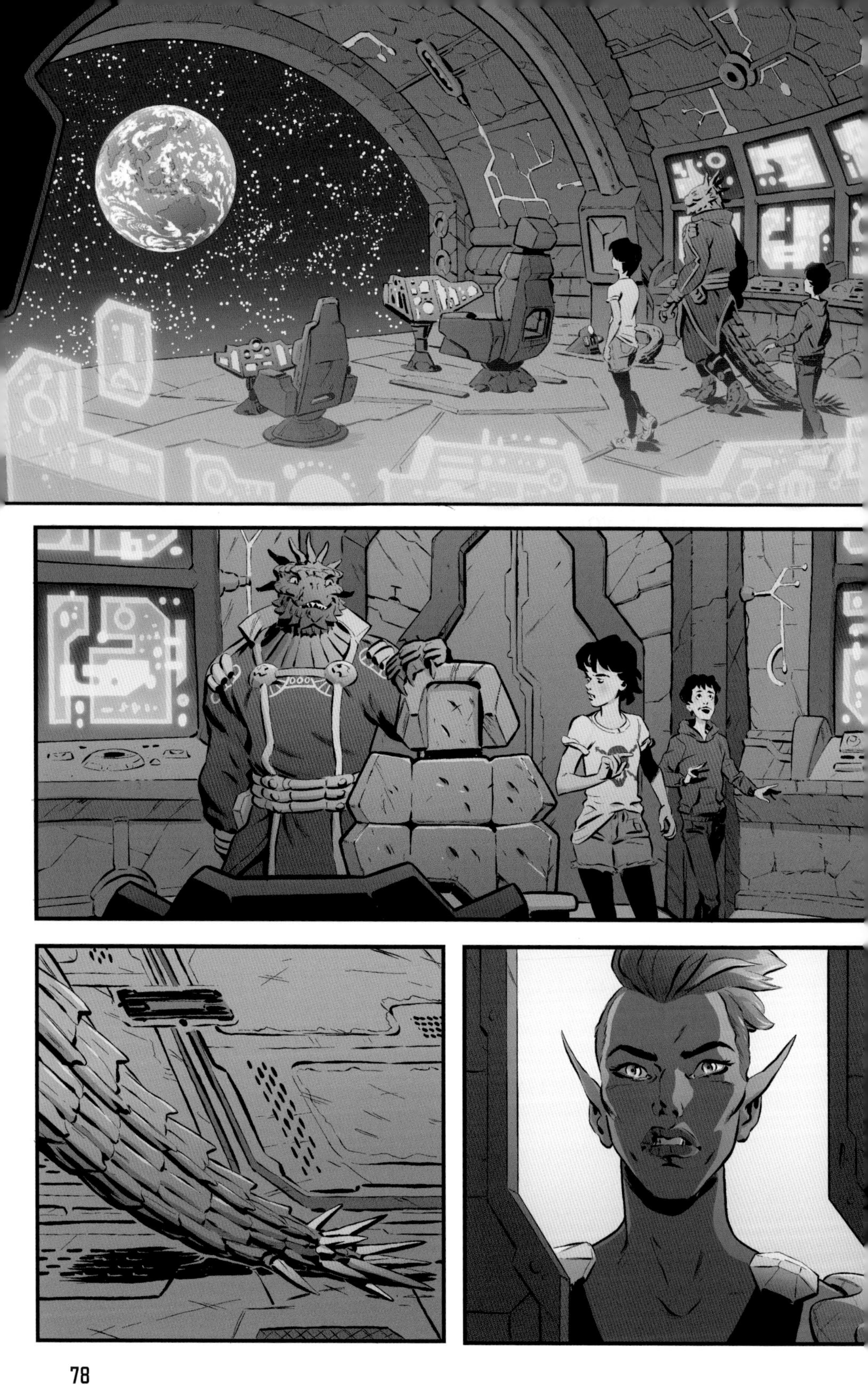

"We were scared you were going to die. It took a while for us to realize that your nanites had been deactivated. I don't know what Parishvi was thinking." She comes closer and studies Alice and Elias with squinting eyes. "Wow! You really are her children. Unmistakable."

"The similarity is truly striking," says Brock, and adds in a slightly quieter voice: "Or so Arisa tells me."

"Hang on! You know Mom?" says Alice.

"Of course," says Syndra.

Hope flutters in her chest. Maybe, just maybe, everything is going to be OK.

"Do you know where she is?"

"No. We followed an encrypted signal, hoping it would lead us to her. But instead we found you."

Alice's hope vanishes as quickly as it appeared.

"How do you know her?" Elias asks.

"What do you mean?" says Syndra.

"Well… you're aliens. You come from outer space."

"Didn't she tell you?" says Syndra, surprised.

"What?" says Alice.

"Your mother is also from outer space."

ALICE

Alice realizes she's standing with her mouth wide open. She looks over at Elias who is equally shocked.

"What do you mean?" he says to Syndra. "Mom's an… alien?"

"We don't call ourselves aliens," says Brock. "But from your perspective, yes."

Syndra takes something green and round out of her trouser pocket. It's the sensor Alice took out of the tree. Before that creature appeared. Before life turned completely upside down.

"This is where the signal came from. Maybe there's more it can tell us."

Syndra walks up to the wall, folds down something that looks like a round glass bowl and puts the box inside.

"What's…" Alice begins.

"It's a reader," says Syndra.

"I mean the plastic box. You said it sent out a signal."

"It's a hyper-transmitter."

Alice and Elias must look confused, because Syndra shakes her head and continues.

"Dark filth of the abyss! You really do live on a primitive planet. These things send messages through hyperspace. Faster than the speed of light. Without it she would never have been able to contact us."

"So Mom sent you a message?"

"Yes. She asked us to come. Said she needed help."

Arisa's voice sounds throughout the bridge.

"Analyzing the hyper-transmitter. The memory bank is encrypted. One moment… Encryption breached. There are no sent messages. Someone must have erased them. However, there is one new message, intended for sending but never sent because it lacks the required signature."

"Play it!" says Brock.

Alice gives a start. It's Mom's voice. She's in distress. Her voice sounds so clear as if she's standing right next to them. She's speaking a language Alice has never heard before, but knows it is Galactic Standard Three. But how? Those nanites again. They're translating and she understands every word.

"I've been captured! The Krao, those snakes! They've cut my arm off!" Mom gasps for air and then collects herself again. "Madukar! I heard them speaking. Madukar is the name of their mothership. They're loading me onto the shuttle now. Brock, if you hear this: find out who the ship belongs to. Find out who hired them! And whatever you do, make sure…"

There is a bang, a snap, and then everything goes quiet.

Elias has gone white as a sheet. His delight of being on a spaceship evaporated. Alice puts her arms around him. She can feel herself shaking, too. Mom has been taken prisoner by those monsters.

"They cut off her arm!" Elias says flatly, as if he can't grasp his own words.

"That's no big deal," says Syndra. "It'll grow back."

Alice stares at her, trying to understand the lunacy coming out of her mouth.

"What do you mean grow back? Her arm?"

Syndra looks back at her incomprehensibly.

"Yes. Don't yours do that?"

Alice holds one hand up in front of her and wiggles her fingers.

"Not usually. It's not normal."

"So if someone on your planet gets a finger chopped off they go through the rest of their life without that finger?"

"Yes."

Syndra rolls her eyes.

"Just when I thought you couldn't get any more primitive."

Brock opens his mouth only slightly, but enough to show his sharp teeth and lets out a low, disapproving growl.

"Yes, yes. Sorry. I didn't mean to speak badly of your simple dump of a home planet."

"Syndra!" Brock snaps.

"Sorry, sorry."

"So why do you have a metal arm?" Elias asks and points.

"Because I want to," says Syndra.

"Can't you make a new one grow out again?"

"I can. But I chose not to."

Brock walks over to the transmitter box and studies it with his yellow reptilian eyes.

"The Krao were loading her onto a shuttle. She probably had a commlink in her pocket and got a final message to the hyper-transmitter. But the Krao must have discovered what she was doing and stopped her before she could sign off the message. So it got stuck in the hyper-transmitter's buffer." He drums his claw on the box thoughtfully. "The Krao didn't want to leave any trace behind. That's why they were hunting you in the woods."

Alice shivers. She pictures the raised knife in front of her. Those big black eyes.

"Who are they?" she asks. "Who's taken my mom?"

Syndra glances at Brock and he nods back as if to say: "You tell them." She sighs.

"Arisa, show us a Krao."

The Earth and stars disappear. The large hologram screen comes loose from the wall, floats into the room and morphs into a long, thin shape. A moment later, the creature from

Alice's horrific chase in the woods is standing right in front of them.

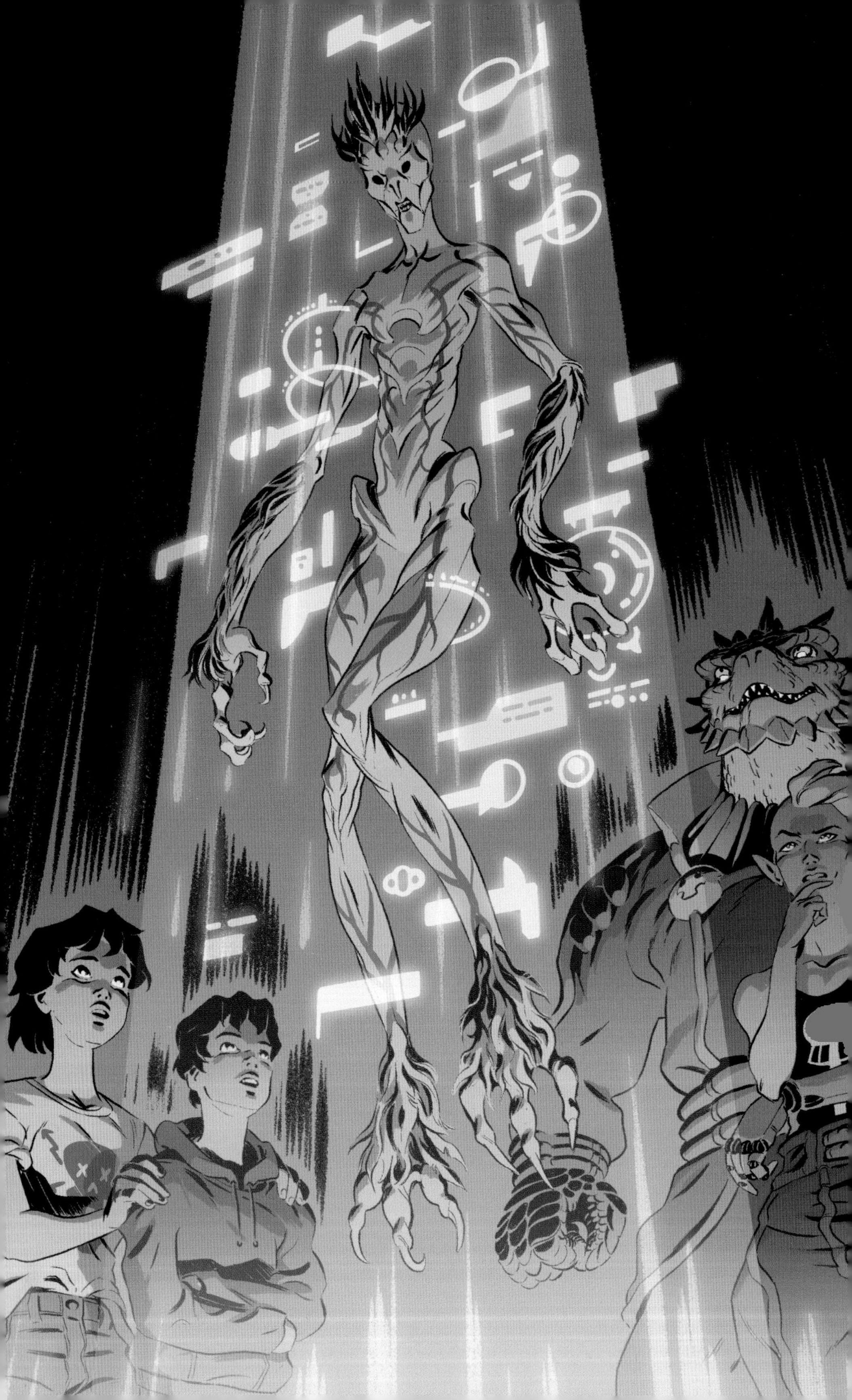

ALICE

"This is a Krao," says Syndra.

The creature in front of them rotates slowly so Alice can see it from all directions. It has two arms and two legs and is almost human-shaped, but not quite. Its skin is patterned and shifts between green, yellow, and purple. She might have thought it was beautiful if she weren't so angered by the sight of it.

Its face is just as she remembers. The narrow mouth is closed, but she knows it has sharp teeth inside. On its head it has a crown of feathers, or is it hair? Hard to tell. The arms are slightly too long, with four fingers on each hand. The legs are also longer than a human's and angled differently. Instead of feet it has three claws at the end of its legs, covered with the same kind of feathery hair.

"They were driven from their home planet over 3,000 years ago," continues Syndra. "Since then, they have been forced to drift through the galaxy. They are skilled warriors, so they are often employed as mercenaries. But once the battles are fought, their employers want nothing to do with them, so they continue travelling. They are never really welcome anywhere, and are constantly moving from star to star."

"That sounds awful," says Alice.

Then she stops herself. If these creatures have taken her mother, they don't deserve her pity. But still, it does sound like they are forced to live pretty horrible lives.

"Why can't they just settle down on some planet and stay there?" Elias says.

Brock laughs.

"Most habitable planets are already full of people. And do you have any idea how expensive it is to terraform a new world?"

"What is… terraform?"

Syndra giggles loudly.

"By the spawn of the dark gods! What has Parishvi been playing at? You don't know anything!"

"Hush," says Brock. "We have no idea what she was planning. Maybe the idea was to live like those earthlings do, and never leave the planet."

"And live her whole life on the same forgotten lump of rock?" Syndra lashes out angrily. "Preventing her children from travelling between the stars, seeing new suns rise across alien worlds, talking to other intelligent beings and learning how they think, smelling the scent of rare flowers, eating strange and wonderful foods? They are Alonai! Sure, they grew up on a primitive planet and are bizarrely pale, but they are Alonai nonetheless. It's their privilege to travel through the galaxy! She has denied them their birthright!"

Elias turns defiantly to Syndra.

"Our mother loves us!" he says. "She's always taken good care of us. Right, Alice?"

Alice just nods. There is a big lump in her throat.

She points to the still-rotating hologram of the Krao and says, "Can you show us pictures of Mom? Before she came to Earth."

"I have a large number of portraits in my database from the period she spent as captain of the Phoenix," says Arisa.

The Krao disappears and several dozen photos of mom pop up on the holographic screen instead. It's definitely her, but she looks different.

Alice blinks several times. Mom has blue skin.

Just like Syndra. Two bright golden eyes shine from her blue face, and two pointed ears stick out through her glossy green hair.

Elias stares open-mouthed.

"So…" says Alice. "Mom was blue."

"Yes," says Arisa.

"And now she's not."

"Apparently not."

"How did she get rid of her blue skin? And the pointed ears? And everything else?"

"In all likelihood, she killed her photosynthetic cells and had her ears rounded with cosmetic surgery," says Arisa. "Medically speaking it isn't hard to do."

Alice and Elias look questioningly at the ceiling.

Arisa clears her throat like a schoolteacher about to explain something complex to her students:

"The Alonai have a layer of photosynthetic cells in their skin that allows them to absorb sunlight from a wide variety of star types. The cells are blue, which is why their skin is blue. The green plants on Earth also live on sunlight, though probably use a different substance, which I know nothing about."

"Chlorophyll," says Alice. "The plants on Earth use chlorophyll. That's what makes them green."

So she did learn something in her science youth group after all.

"Wait a minute," says Elias. "Photosynthesis? Are the Alonai plants?"

Syndra laughs.

"Do you think I look like a vegetable?"

"No, but…"

"It's a survival thing," says Syndra. "Of course I prefer to eat regular food, but if I were to end up on a hostile planet I could survive for weeks, maybe months, on nothing but water and sunbathing."

Elias bursts into a wide smile.

"Cool!"

Alice doesn't care about Syndra's photosynthetic skin. She looks at the holographic images.

"So Mom was the captain?"

"Yes," says Arisa.

"Of this ship?"

"Yes."

"What do you do? I mean, how do you make money?"

"We are bounty hunters."

"What, so you chase bad guys for cash?"

"Yes."

"Dead or alive?" Elias asks. His eyes shining.

"Yes."

"So cool!"

Alice wants to kick him in the shin. Hard. But she restrains herself.

"When did Mom leave the Phoenix?" she asks instead.

"Fifteen years ago."

"Fifteen years!" Alice repeats. "That's when she came to Sweden."

"From Vietnam," says Elias.

They look at each other. No, obviously not from Vietnam.

Alice has a bitter taste in her mouth. She hates this. All she wants is to be back home, to lounge on the sofa and hear

Mom dawdling around in her workshop in the basement and Dad cooking in the kitchen. But that's all gone, and it feels like there's a big hole in her chest.

"That explains why she always refused to go to Vietnam to visit our grandparents," she says. "They don't exist. She has probably not even been there. She has been lying to us all these years."

Elias pushes out his lower lip. She can see that he is going into defensive mode. He doesn't want to think badly of mom.

"She didn't lie," he says. "She just didn't tell the whole truth. That's not the same thing."

Alice tries to laugh it off because she can't bear an argument, but her laughter sounds hollow.

"Yes, maybe you're right."

Elias takes her hand.

"What would she have said?" he continues. "By the way kids, just so you know: I'm really a pointy-eared blue space alien."

"We would never have believed her."

"I wonder if Dad knows."

Alice thinks of Dad's sad face in the garage. How worried he was that Mom still hadn't come home.

"No, I don't think so."

Then the door to the bridge opens and a giant bird walks in.

ALICE

The sight of the bird creature startles Alice, causing her to stumble backwards and almost trip over her feet. She barely manages to keep from falling.

The bird is tall, probably seven feet. Its feathers shift from reddish brown to white, but the feathers at the crest and around the eyes shine blue. Halfway along the wings, in the same place as a bat has its claws, are long, sharp talons.

"Glad you're here, Farei," says Brock. "Let me introduce you to the children."

"Yes, Captain." The bird creature bobs its head and stands in front of Elias and Alice with its sharp beak and big red eyes. It might have been scary if its eyes weren't so kind.

Brock holds a hand out to the bird and makes a very proud introduction.

"This is Farei of Kehkaga, one of the best pilots in all of the Sickle. We are very happy to have her on board."

Alice notices two things. First, how much Farei appreciates Brock's praise. She stands up tall and puffs out her feathers. Second, that Elias doesn't seem in the least bit surprised at the revelation.

"Do you know that bird?" she whispers to her brother.

Elias doesn't whisper back. He answers loudly.

"Yeah, Farei was flying the shuttle when they lifted us off the ground."

Alice doesn't remember any shuttle; all she remembers is the light, the all-encompassing light, raising her high above the treetops.

Elias nods to Farei.

"Thank you for helping me and my sister. I know you tried talking to me, but that was before I got those nanite things in my brain activated. So I didn't understand anything."

Farei does an elegant bow and emits a musical whirl of twitters and trills.

"It was the least I could do," the nanites translate. "It was an honor to fly two Alonai to safety and I offer you my wings whenever you wish."

Alice just stares at the bird. She understood exactly what she was saying, even though the sounds she made were nothing close to anything recognizable as speech. Those nanites are absolutely incredible!

"I have a question," says Elias.

"Just one?" asks Alice. Elias doesn't seem to hear her.

"Where are you from?" he begins. "Are there more of you out there? How many planets are actually inhabited by aliens? Why don't we know anything about you on Earth?"

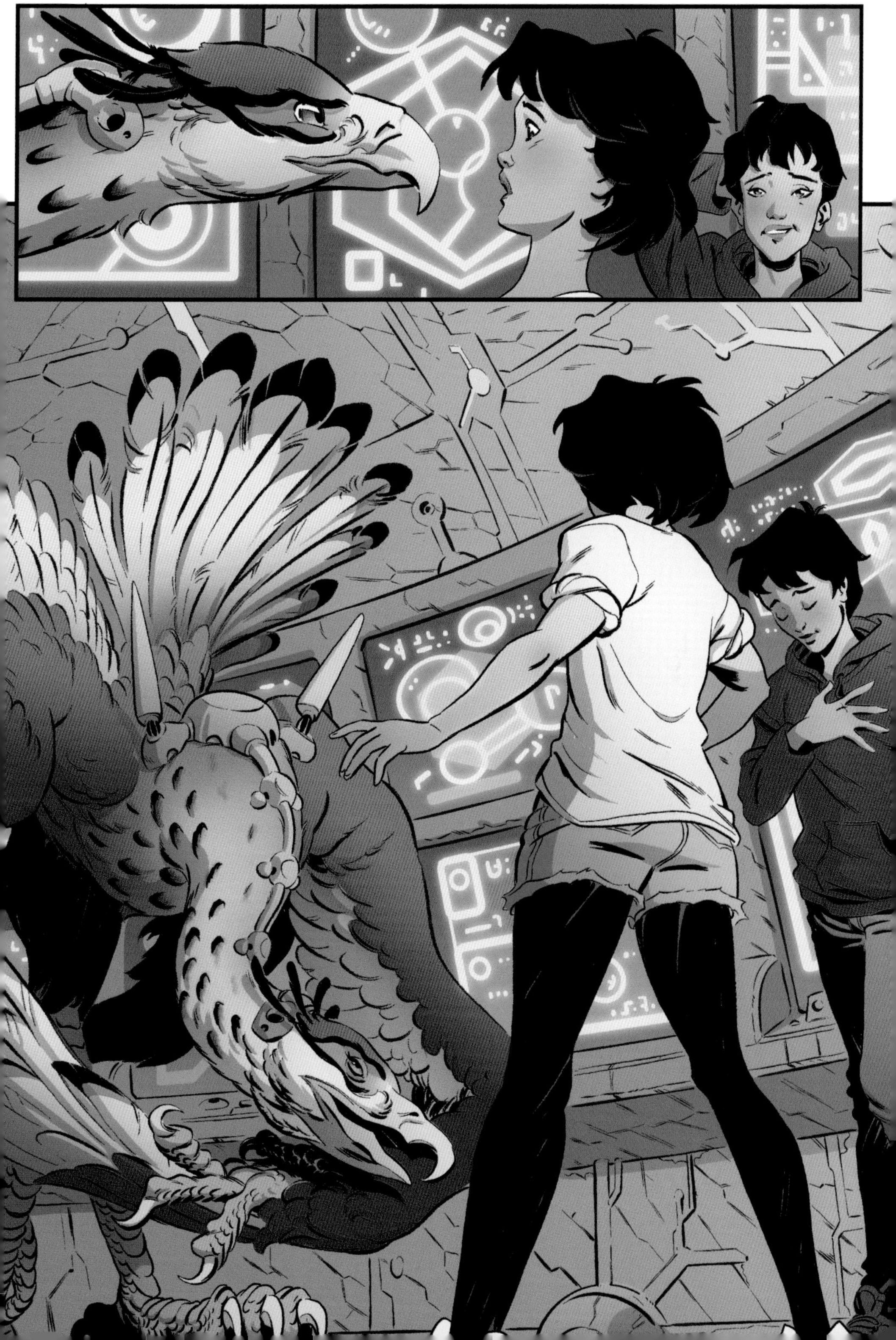

"That was a lot of questions," says Alice, raising her eyebrows pointedly.

Farei stretches out her wings.

"I'm a Vrok, young man. I come from the planet Rikva, the home world of all Vrok."

Brock clears his throat and pats himself on the chest. "And I'm an Azkalor," he says. Alice notices that Farei beams on seeing the captain follow her example.

"Personally, I come from the planet Zerbum. But we Azkalor have tens of thousands of worlds across the galaxy. We are an ancient race. We've travelled among the stars for so long that no one really knows where we originated from. Our true home world is lost in the mists of time. Only songs and myths remain."

Farei bows reverently to Brock.

"The Azkalor are known throughout the galaxy as the Eternal Ones," she says. "They have always been here and watched over us younger races."

But Brock doesn't seem too happy on hearing Farei's words. On the contrary, Alice thinks she sees sadness in his eyes.

"How many are you in the crew?" Elias asks.

"Once you've met Kapa, our mechanic, you'll have met everyone," says Syndra.

Elias counts on his fingers.

"So you, Brock, Farei and Kapa. Only four?"

CHAPTER 15

"Don't forget Arisa," says Syndra. "She may be a synthetic life form – not biological like the rest of us – but she is an important part of the crew."

"Thank you. It makes me happy that you remembered me," Arisa's voice is heard from the ceiling.

"Of course," says Syndra. "You are the heart of the Phoenix. We wouldn't survive two seconds without you."

Alice feels a huge yawn rising up through her body and forcing its way out of her mouth. Elias yawns immediately after.

"I think we've talked enough for tonight," says Syndra. "Come on, I'll show you to your cabin."

The cabin is small and cold. It reminds Alice of a broom cupboard. Except a broom cupboard usually contains a lot of stuff: mops, buckets, wash cloths and such. In here there is nothing. Just bare metal walls.

"I apologize for the modest furnishings," says Syndra. "But the Phoenix is a small ship and this is the only cabin available at the moment. We weren't exactly planning on picking up hitch-hikers."

"But where are we supposed to sleep?" Alice asks. "On the floor?"

Syndra smiles.

"No, no, of course not."

She touches a white plastic wall panel.

"Two beds," she says.

The wall panel softens at once like a mass of molten plastic and swells out into the room. Then it starts to change shape. It pulls together, forms sharp edges and… as if by magic, a bunk bed appears before them. It looks as ordinary as any they might see at home on Earth.

They hear a loud whooshing sound as two mattresses are inflated. One end of the mattress has a raised lump like a pillow.

"Do you have any duvets?" Alice asks.

"Duvets?"

"Something to cover us."

Syndra waves her hand dismissively.

"The ship's atmosphere is heated to the ideal temperature so you won't be cold."

"It would still be nice to have something to cover ourselves with. We're used to it. It helps us sleep better."

Syndra shrugs.

"I'll find something. And you'll need clothes to sleep in, too."

She takes a step to leave, but stops. "I know you didn't choose this, that you would prefer to just go home. But I promise that tomorrow we will find the Krao ship. We will find your mother and we will set her free." She looks Alice and then Elias in the eye. "I promise."

ALICE

Alice lies in her new bunk bed and stares up at the ceiling. She's wearing the nightdress Syndra gave her. Elias got the same. Apparently, all Alonai wear nightdresses. Syndra also managed to get hold of some kind of blankets. They're large and fluffy.

There is no lamp in the room. Then again, she has not seen a single lamp since she woke up on the Phoenix. Instead a warm, uniform light glows from the ceiling. Right now the light is dimmed like dusk. She really wants to ask Arisa to turn it off completely, but she knows that Elias doesn't like total darkness. He still sleeps with a night light and she doesn't want him to wake up and feel scared. Alice has no idea what time it is. She should be dead tired considering everything that has happened but she's full of nervous energy.

Her fingers reach for her phone, but then she remembers that it's still somewhere in Lunsen, by the big rock where the creature attacked her. She shudders at the memory.

Elias moves in the bed beneath her.

"Are you awake?" she whispers.

"Yes."

She lies there quietly for a while. She tries to put her thoughts into words. About how bizarre this all is. How much she misses Mom and Dad.

"I just wish I could brush my teeth," says Elias.

Alice bursts into giggles.

"Seriously? We're on a spaceship with these crazy aliens and a talking computer and you've been told that you have microscopic robots in your body – and you miss your toothbrush?"

"Yes. Having nanites clean your mouth isn't the same. It makes my gums itch. And it doesn't taste of anything. I miss my minty toothpaste."

"You're nuts."

"Maybe. But you're wrong. "

"About what?"

"About the others on the ship. They're not crazy. They're nice. And they care. We can trust them."

"You think so? They might sell us as slaves on the next planet they land. Or as meat for some galactic burger chain."

"Joke all you want. But they are kind, even though they look big and dangerous."

"How can you be so sure?"

"They're Mom's friends."

"No, they were Mom's friends. A long time ago. That doesn't mean anything now."

"I trust them anyway."

They're quiet for a while, both awake.

Alice looks up at the ceiling. She feels that gaping hole in her chest again.

She feels as if she is going to be sucked into it, and disappear bit by bit until nothing is left.

"Alice," Elias says suddenly. "I think I know why the police took Dad."

She feels a jolt pass through her body and suddenly it becomes hard to breathe. The memory of the police leading Dad out the door.

"Those idiots!" she exclaims. "Just because they had a fight. Sure, there might be little blood in the car, but–"

Elias interrupts her.

"That's not why. It was something else. I knew it when we were talking to that police officer, Frida. She knew something she wasn't saying, and now I've figured out what it was."

"What?"

"They must have found an arm. Mom's arm…" Elias' voice breaks but he continues anyway. "She said in that message that the Krao cut her arm off…" He sniffs and clears his throat. "If it was out there in Lunsen then somebody must have found it, a jogger or one of those dog walkers who are always out in the woods."

"But how would they know it was her arm?"

"Maybe she was the only person reported missing. No, wait!" Elias always gets enthusiastic when solving mysteries. Even something as morbid as this. "That must be it! If it was her left arm, then her wedding ring would be on that hand. Then it would be easy to find out who she is."

"And arms don't grow back on Earth," Alice muses. "If the police find an arm in the forest, they expect the person to be dead."

"Exactly. So they think she's been murdered."

Alice tries to breathe. Tries not to think about how awful it all is.

"Poor Dad," says Elias. He sounds like he is crying.

"And now we've disappeared as well!" says Alice.

"Exactly," Elias says. "What's he going to think when his children disappear without a trace, too? But wait, now they'll have to let him go."

"Why?"

"Because they'll know it wasn't him."

"They'll know he didn't do anything to us. But they can't rule out he's not responsible for Mom's disappearance."

Elias thinks about it for a few seconds.

"Do you think he'll go to jail?"

"I don't know."

They go quiet again. Alice misses her parents so much it hurts, but she feels something else too, something that gives her strength. She's seething with anger. This is all so incredibly unfair – on Dad, on Mom, on all of them. And it fills her with determination.

"We have to save Dad, too."

"Yes."

"The only way to save him is by rescuing Mom. Only she can prove his innocence."

"And she's on that ship."

"Yes. As Syndra said, we will find it, and we'll free her."

"Yes, we will."

Fatigue catches up with them. Alice wants to sleep now. But the bed isn't like hers at home, it doesn't have the right dips for her body to sink into.

"Can I sleep next to you?" she asks.

"Yeah, come down."

Elias sounds almost relieved.

She quickly climbs down and creeps in beside him. They put their arms around each other and pull the blanket up. The bed feels new and different, but Elias' body is warm and familiar.

"Elias," she says, "can you sing Mom's lullaby again? The one… you know."

Elias knows the one she means. He starts to sing, quietly but clearly, and she joins in.

The Phoenix travels through space at night
With five horns on its head
Sleep my two and enjoy her journey
Let the dream come true
Seven came
Two came
Four sheep came
Let's count them
Three came
Five came
Eight sheep came
Manna rains from heaven
No one can see the future
Keep the song inside you
No, no one can see the future
Keep the song inside you.

They lie in silence for a while.

"Hey," she says, "It's actually a really weird song. Just a bunch of words that don't make sense."

"Well that's lullabies for you," says Elias. "The one that Dad used to sing about a goose doesn't make much sense either. Goosey goosey gander and all that."

Alice laughs.

"No, you're right."

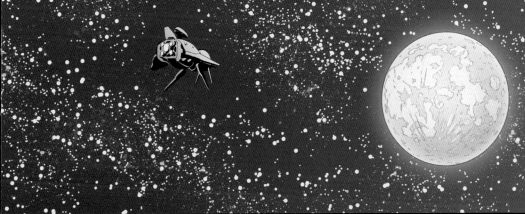

"Good night," says Elias.

"Night."

But it's a while before she falls asleep.

ALICE

Alice wakes up to the sound of a siren and has no idea how long they've been asleep. The alarm is so loud it makes her head rattle. She instinctively jumps out of bed and starts putting on her regular clothes.

"Is there a fire?" Elias says sleepily, rubbing his eyes.

"I don't know."

Is a fire even possible on a spaceship? She takes a quick look around their little cabin. There isn't much that can catch fire in here anyway, just their clothes, and maybe the blankets.

"We have to find out what's going on! Get dressed!"

Elias gets up and starts putting on his jeans and sweater.

Then the alarm goes silent and Arisa's voice is heard from the ceiling.

"All crew members to the bridge! Unidentified ship detected. This is a code red, I repeat, code red."

Alice pushes the button that opens the cabin door and they burst out into the corridor. They almost collide with Brock.

"Excuse me," he says as he swerves smoothly around them, despite his large frame, and continues towards the bridge. He's sprinting as though he's being chased by a giant hairy monster. Though Alice has a hard time believing that Brock would be afraid of a big hairy monster… It would more likely be the other way around.

"Let's go!" she says.

"But we're not part of the crew," says Elias.

Alice just tuts and speeds towards the bridge. Elias follows.

She comes in through the door just as Brock leaps into his captain's chair. He effortlessly wiggles his tail through the gap in the backrest with his eyes fixed on the holographic screen on the wall. His tail begins to thrash against the floor.

Farei comes in behind them, flapping her wings and hovering around the room. She lands softly on the branch in the floor and digs her claws in, leaning her head and body forward and moving her talons across the panel at lightning speed.

Alice thinks that Farei looks a bit like a skier in a downhill race. But with feathers.

Syndra also appears and rushes to her chair.

"Arisa! What's going on? What kind of ship is that?" growls Brock.

CHAPTER 17

Arisa's voice projects throughout the bridge.

"I don't know. But it's heading straight for us."

BROCK

Brock feels the scales on his chest contract into a defensive position in anticipation of an attack. He tries to shake it off and relax.

"I have the ship on sensor," says Syndra. "It's close. Very close!"

"Why didn't we see it before?"

"It was hidden behind the moon. It must have been there the whole time, even when we landed on Earth."

The holo-screen shifts and the moon appears. The picture zooms in to show a huge black ship. It looks harsh and angular, with sharp edges and huge spikes.

"Do we know who they are?" Brock asks.

"No, they're not transmitting an identification signal," says Arisa.

"They have a statue of Krokcha on top," says Syndra.

"Then it's one of the war clans," says Brock.

"But which one? Scan it. I want to know what kind of ship it is and who it belongs to."

"Scanning."

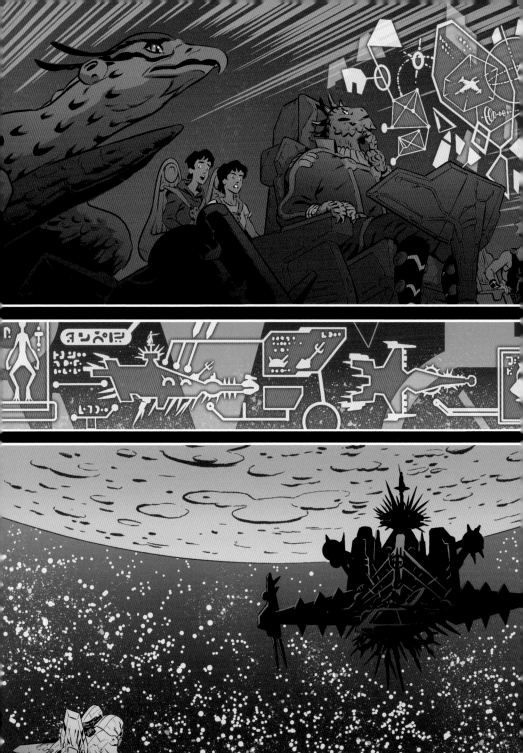

"They're raising their shields," says Syndra. "They're preparing to fight!"

"Raise ours too," Brock commands.

A whining sound pulsates through the hull of the Phoenix as the shield generators start up. The whine grows louder and more high pitched until it goes beyond his range of hearing.

It's time for their star pilot to take control of the Phoenix. Arisa is a very competent AI and is often left to control the ship. But in battle, they need someone who can steer with the kind of creativity and unpredictability that keeps the enemy guessing. They need a Vrok.

"Farei, plug in."

Farei nods and flicks her tail feathers. Her long talons pull the neuro cable out of its compartment in the terminal and push it into a jack in her neck. She closes her eyes. The cable is thin and looks almost flimsy, but it connects Farei's thoughts directly to the mainframe of the Phoenix. Now the large bird of prey is controlling the ship as if it were her own body.

"They're scanning us," Arisa says.

Brock squints, studying the contours of the alien ship.

"Call them."

Syndra pushes a few buttons.

"No answer," she says. "They don't seem to want to communicate."

"Their weapon system?"

"They are ready to fire missiles, but their energy weapons are not warmed up. Yet."

"Arisa. Is Kapa ready in the engine room?"

"What do you mean? He's in hibernation."

Brock swears quietly. How could he have forgotten?

"Wake him up! It's an emergency!"

"I'll try."

"Get him up. We need him now!"

"I'm getting no response. You know how heavily Troggs sleep when they hibernate."

"Keep trying!"

The ship on the holo-screen moves closer. The ship's strange angles seem to be due to it having been built from parts of several other vessels, possibly salvaged from a space junkyard. Typical of the Krao. They use whatever they can get their hands on. And the ship is huge!

"They're supplying energy to the guns," says Syndra. "They'll be ready soon!"

Brock smiles. His lips pull back and his long blue tongue darts in and out between his teeth. He feels a sudden hunger, like a predator about to devour its enemy.

"Do the same," he says. "But do not fire. Let them shoot first."

"Roger."

Brock stares at the enemy ship. By the ancestors, it's so big! The Phoenix is fast and well-armed for its size, but it's not designed to go up against a beast like this.

His mind is racing and the scales on his chest contract again. He tries to quiet his mind. Think clearly. See the big picture.

"That could be the Krao ship that Parishvi mentioned," he says. "Madukar. Maybe that's where they're keeping her captive."

"Do you really think so?" says a squeaky voice.

Brock turns his head and looks down at the pale little Alonai. The boy is staring transfixed at the misshapen silhouette on the holo-screen.

"Your mother might be a prisoner on that ship," says Brock, "Or she might be somewhere else. Either way, we have to find out which clan the ship belongs to."

Parishvi's children. They stand there wide-eyed, holding hands. So pitifully small and unprepared for the dangers awaiting them out here. Brock feels an itch between his horns. He raises his claw to scratch over his skull. He has a decision to make and it's not easy. He clenches his jaws together and his tail hits the floor.

"This is far too dangerous for you," he says and then turns to Syndra. "Put them in an escape pod and send them back to Earth."

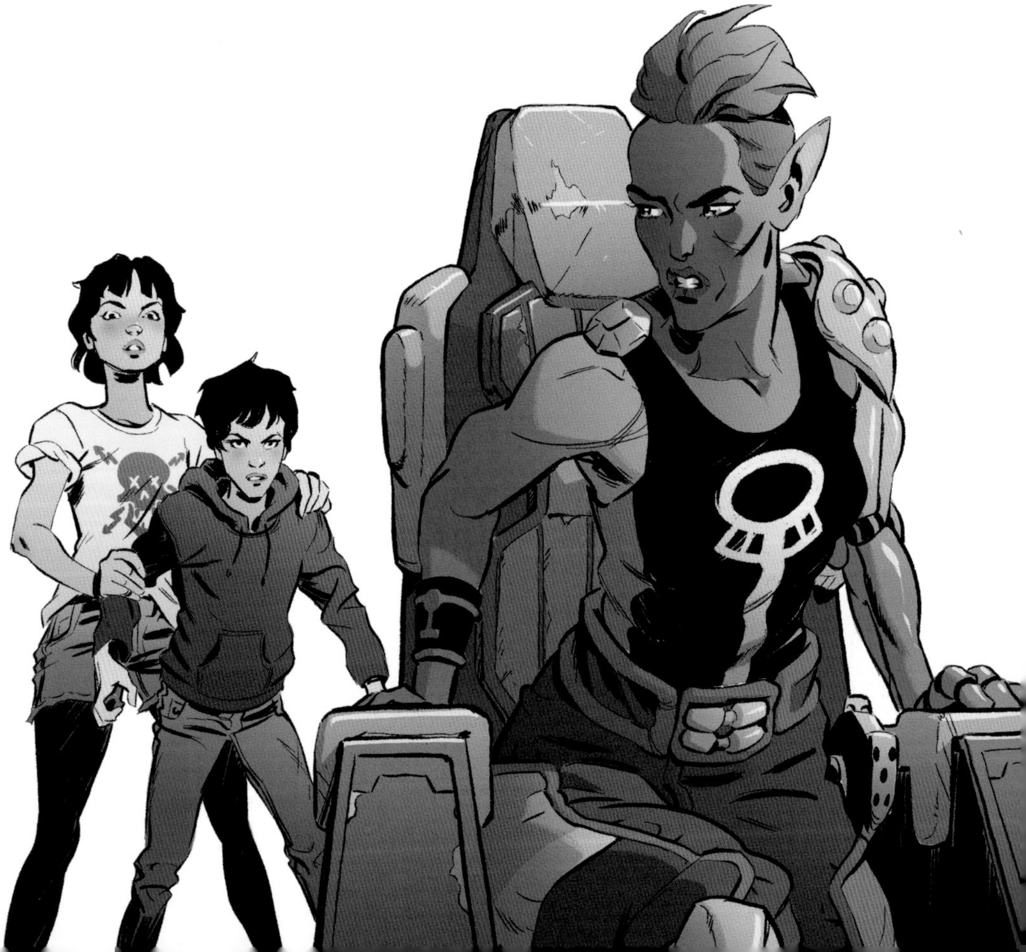

ALICE

Alice can't believe her ears. Brock can't be serious. But Syndra gets up immediately and steps towards them, intending to seize them with her metal arm and force them off the Phoenix.

"No!" Alice screams, taking a step back. "If Mom is on that ship, I have to rescue her!" She puts her arm around Elias' shoulders. "We have to save her!"

Syndra stops and looks at Brock.

"Look, I know they're only children. But it doesn't feel right to send them away like this."

"If they stay, there's a risk they will die," replies Brock.

"But it might not be safe for them down on Earth, either. A Krao tried to kill the girl. Some of those lowlifes might be waiting to kill them as soon as they get home."

Brock looks at Alice. She feels like his reptilian eyes are boring into her skull. She looks away.

"You have to decide for yourselves," he says. "Back to the life you know on Earth… or join us."

"We're coming with you," says Alice. She tries to sound

strong and determined, but her voice barely holds. Part of her wants to run into that escape pod and plunge back down to Earth, back to her old life.

Except that life no longer exists, she reminds herself.

"I'm staying, too," says Elias. His voice is steadier than hers. He stares Brock straight in the eye.

The big lizard tilts his head and turns to face the control panel.

"OK. You can stay."

Alice lets out a breath she didn't know she was holding. She looks at Elias, and he looks back and nods.

"It wouldn't be right to go home," he says, almost solemnly.

Deep down, she feels the same way. This is where they're supposed to be. Even if it's dangerous.

"Arisa," says Syndra. "Two extra seats please."

"Straight away."

Part of the floor in front of them suddenly changes shape and grows upward. In a matter of seconds the mass morphs into a small sofa with room for two people, complete with seat belts and everything.

"Sit down," says Syndra. "By all the Ruptors and their slithering tentacles, you'd better put your seat belts on."

They barely have time to sit down and figure out how the belts work before Farei shouts:

"They're shooting!"

CHAPTER 19

On the holo-screen they see the unidentified ship open fire. Red and yellow streaks of light shoot out and strike the Phoenix's shield. Half a second later, the Phoenix responds with beams of light torpedoing through the darkness. Powerful beams attack the enemy's circular force field, which shimmers blue, green, and yellow. When the force field is touched, it begins to vibrate, giving off rainbow-colored cascades of light. It's incredibly beautiful.

"Faster!" Brock commands.

Farei lets out a high war-like cry and the Phoenix launches towards the enemy.

FAREI

The space between the two ships sizzles and seethes as they blast rays of energy at each other with terrifying intensity. Farei is loving it. Her mind is running the Phoenix's control system. She is the ship and the ship is her. She moves it back and forth, spinning, dancing, making them as difficult a target as possible. She can feel the enemy's weapons hitting the shields, the hull creaking and the engines screaming. It's like music to her ears.

But deep inside, she does get scared. So scared that afterwards she might sit in her cabin and tremble for hours on end. Of course, she doesn't tell the rest of the crew. They think she's this fearless, talented pilot who can do anything. And she's happy to let them believe that. And it is partially true, because right now, as the rays of light flash around her, she is as one with the ship, soaring through the immense darkness like the bird of prey she is. She's happy. Nothing else in the universe can elicit this feeling. Nothing!

"Our shields won't last long," says Syndra. Her voice

sounds muffled and distant. "Their ship is larger with stronger weapons and defenses."

"Will the shields hold for a quick fly-by?" Brock asks.

"Perhaps."

Their captain booms with laughter.

"Farei, push the engines to the limit. Get us right up close so we can scan them and see who they are. Then we move off."

"Aye, Captain," Farei says, smiling inside.

It's a complicated operation. She pulls the Phoenix through a hard turn, evens off, and lets the ship swirl forward, like a leaf in the wind at home on Rikva.

"Initiating fly-by!"

She can't help but let out a wild cry as the Phoenix surges towards the other ship. The enemy seems to be having trouble keeping up; more and more of their shots miss their mark.

They're close now. The unidentified craft looms in front of them. It's gigantic.

"Syndra," says Brock. "Prepare to search for life forms!"

"It can be difficult with their shields up."

"Do it anyway."

"Roger."

Then they whoosh right beneath the enemy ship. Farei can almost feel both ships' force fields rub against each other. Scraping, joining, releasing.

Then they've passed. The unidentified ship, dark and

bulky, quickly shrinks behind them. They stop shooting.

Then Farei sees something. Something that shouldn't be. A shadow, barely visible against the starry background. But it's there. A camouflaged torpedo. Seen too late.

Farei is flying into it at full speed.

A terrible explosion causes the whole hull of the Phoenix to shake. There's a bright flash behind her eyelids. Then everything goes black.

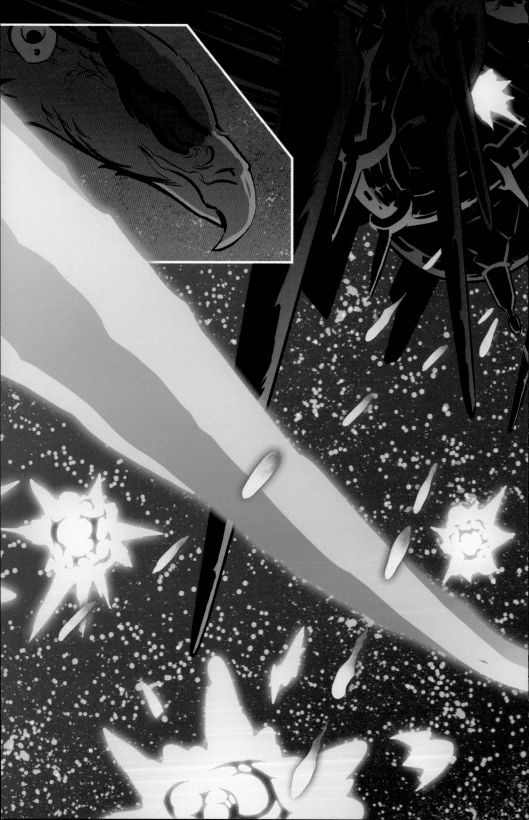

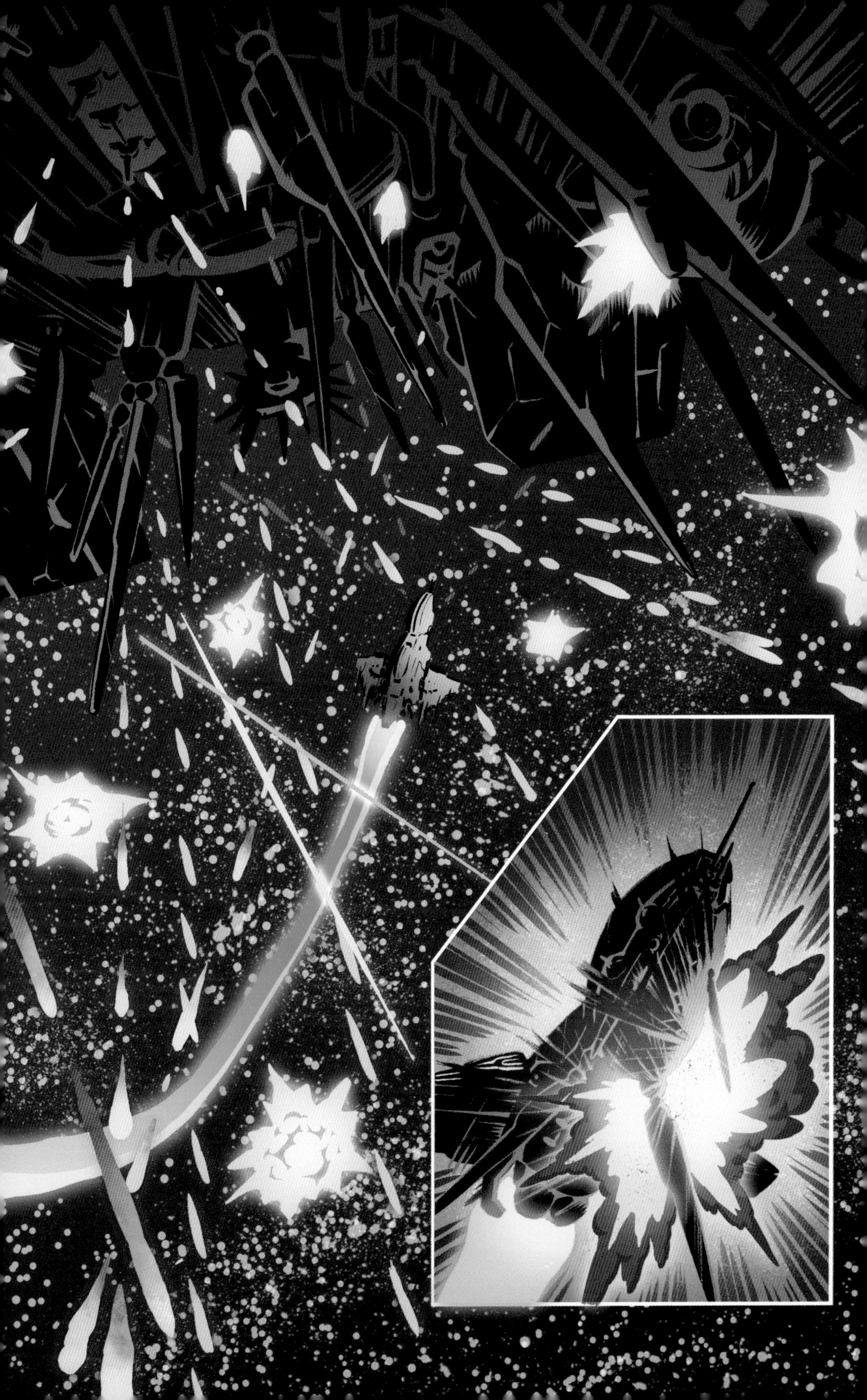

ELIAS

Elias screams in horror. He can't help it. The bridge shuts down. It's pitch dark, not a single speck of light anywhere. Then he feels Alice squeeze his hand. He pauses and takes a deep breath.

"What happened?" Brock shouts into the darkness.

"We've been hit!"

"It must have been a torpedo."

"A torpedo! How did we not see it?"

"Does it matter?"

Brock mutters something inaudible.

"Arisa, what's the damage?" he says.

No answer.

"Arisa?"

Still quiet.

"Oh Ruptors detritus," murmurs Syndra. "Arisa has shut down. The torpedo must have knocked out our computer systems."

Elias fishes his phone out of his pocket and turns on the flashlight. In its glow, he sees Brock and Syndra pounding on their blank-screened computer terminals. On the other side of the room, Farei has collapsed to the floor.

"Farei!" screams Syndra.

Brock and Syndra immediately crouch down next to the big bird.

Elias and Alice get out of their seats and follow. Brock gently places Farei's head in his lap and brings a finger to her neck.

"She's alive."

"What happened?" Elias asks.

Syndra pulls at a cable plugged into the bird's neck. The plug comes loose and Syndra throws the cable away. It was some kind of data transmitter, and Farei had it in her skull! Elias shudders at the thought.

"What was that?" he says.

"Farei was linked to the control system of the Phoenix," says Syndra. "When the torpedo struck, she got a shock to the brain."

"Was she steering the ship with her thoughts?"

"Of course. How else would she have done it?"

Elias can't answer. He just stands there staring as the lights suddenly come on again.

"It seems that the emergency lights work," says Syndra, stroking Farei's downy neck. She looks so vulnerable lying there.

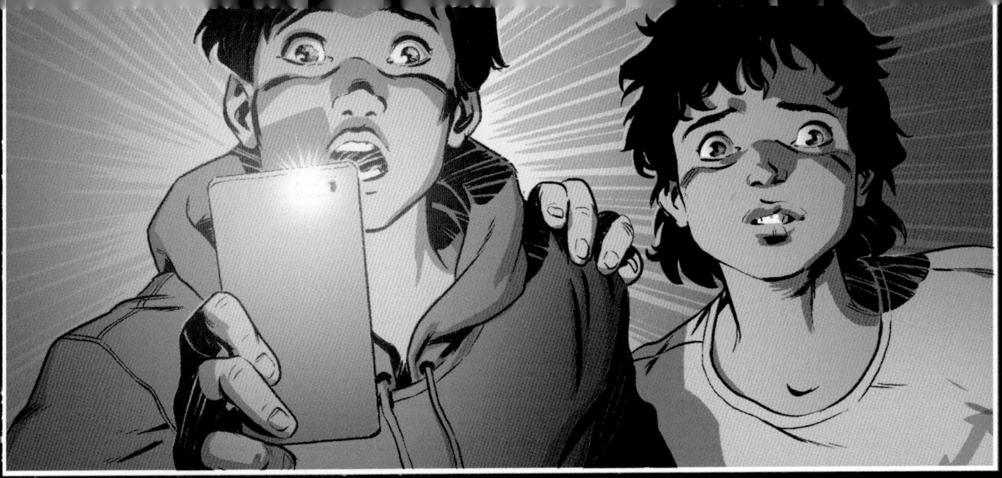
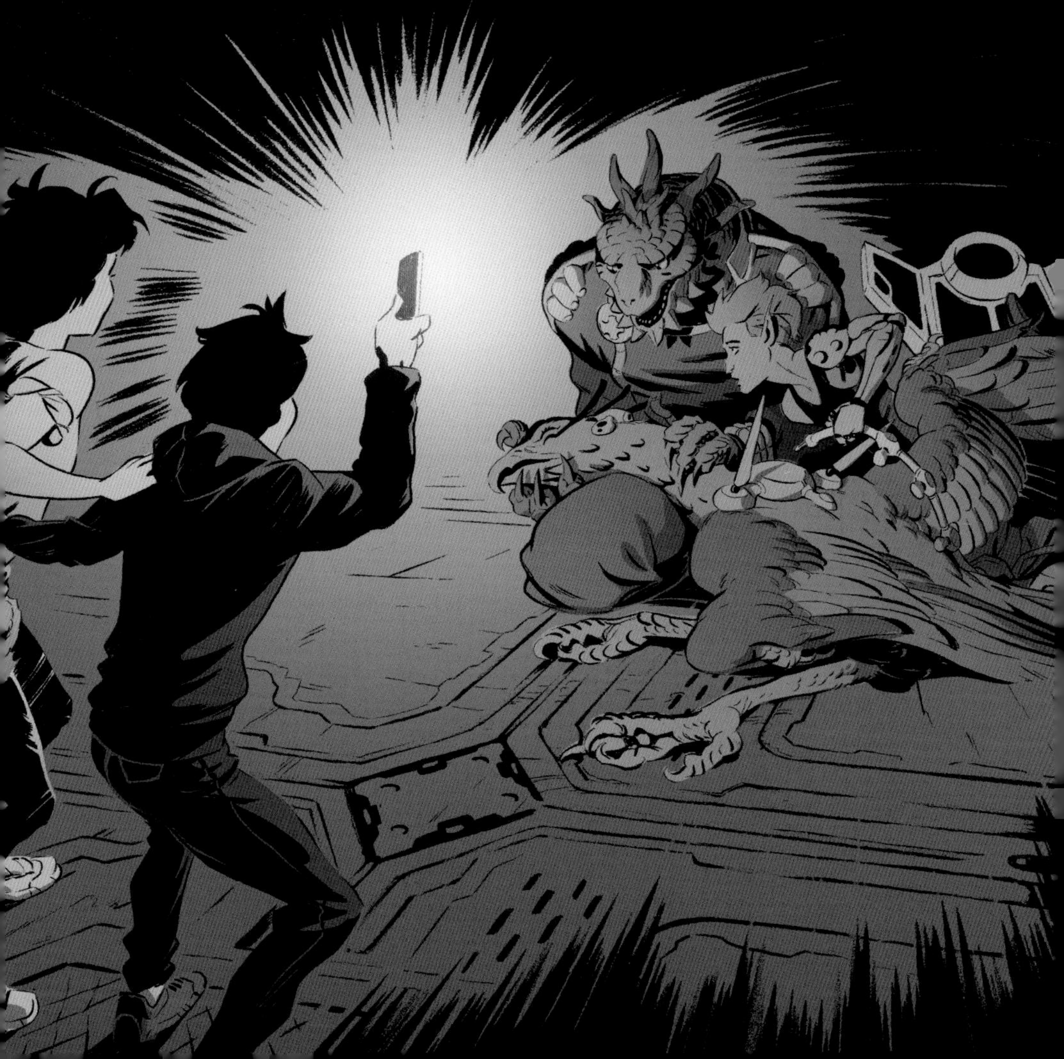

"Arisa?" Brock tries again. "We need help. Farei is seriously injured."

No answer.

"We have to restart Arisa. Without her, we can't operate the engines, shields, or weapons. We're helpless."

"But why haven't they destroyed us already?" says Syndra.

The computer terminals flash. Some screens and holographic symbols appear floating in mid-air. Brock strokes Farei's head before placing it gently on the floor and hurrying back to his seat. He starts pushing buttons like a maniac. Half of them don't seem to do anything.

Elias doesn't really know what to do with himself.

He wants to help Farei, but what does he know about electric shocks to the brain?

"Most of the systems are still down," Brock says after a while. "We have to get to the central computer and restart everything. It's the only way to regain control of the ship."

He pushes a button and the main holo-screen pops up. Brock's eyes narrow.

Elias stares in astonishment at the enormous, bulky ship. It's caught up with the Phoenix, switched off its engines, and is holding a position on a parallel vector, close up. A port opens and a smaller ship, presumably some type of shuttle, glides out. The shuttle races towards the Phoenix.

"That's why they haven't destroyed the Phoenix," says

CHAPTER 21

Brock. "They are going to board us."

"But why?" says Syndra.

"For whatever reason, they want us alive."

"No," says Syndra. She turns around and points to Elias and Alice. "They want the children alive."

ALICE

Alice can hardly breathe. She can feel her knees shaking. Those monsters are on their way here to kidnap her and Elias! Just like they kidnapped Mom. They're going to drag them onto their horrible spaceship and fly them far away into cold, dark space.

Brock stands up tall. It looks as if he's growing right in front of her eyes.

"We have thirteen minutes before the shuttle arrives and they try to board." He meets Syndra's gaze. "I am going to restart the central computer. You take Farei to the sickbay. Hopefully the auto-doctor is still working. And hurry up, we don't know how badly her brain is damaged."

"Roger," says Syndra.

With a grunt, she lifts Farei. The big bird hangs there limply, like an old sack. It pains Alice to see her like that. They've only known each other for a few hours, but still, she likes Farei. She seems so kind.

"Arisa, could you reduce the gravity by…" Syndra goes silent. "Dark mazes of the abyss! One gets so used to her always being there…"

"We'll get her back," says Brock. "Now let's go!"

But the doorway out of the bridge doesn't open. Brock inserts his claws into the central gap and pushes the doors apart with a roar. He disappears into the corridor. Syndra adjusts Farei on her back and rushes after him.

Alice and Elias stare at them. No one has said a word about what they're supposed to do. Should they wait? Should they go with them?

Alice can't just stand there like an idiot doing nothing. Farei is injured, possibly seriously injured. And in thirteen minutes, maybe twelve now, those monsters, those Krao, will storm the Phoenix and take her and Elias. If that happens they will never see Earth again. And she doesn't even want to think about what the Krao will do to the crew.

"We have to help," she says.

Elias just nods. But she recognizes that expression, that determination. He's scared, but he's not going to let that stop him. Dear little brother. She wants to hug him, but there's no time. Instead, she rushes out into the corridor, with Elias close behind. They have to hurry. They have to save the Phoenix.

ALICE

Alice runs with all her might. She gets a sudden feeling of déjà vu, as if she's done this before. And she has. Just a few hours ago, running for her life through Lunsen, chased by that creature. Now she's running again, chased by the same breed of monster, but through empty metal corridors.

She can't see Syndra anywhere, and has forgotten where the sickbay is. But she sees Brock at the far end of the corridor. He's struggling with a massive metal door and yelling like a prehistoric brute, but the door won't budge.

"What's the problem?" she asks as they arrive.

Brock lets go of the door, his tail whipping back and forth in frustration, but he answers clearly, like a soldier giving a report.

"According to this," he says, pointing to a flickering screen next to the door, "there is a fire in the corridor on the other side."

So fires can break out on spaceships.

"The door can't be opened as long as the fire poses a danger," Brock continues. "The system is working exactly as it should.

The only problem is that the central computer is at the other end of that corridor. I have to get in."

"But how are you going to get past the fire even if you do get the door open?" says Alice.

"I'll run."

"And how are you going to open the door at the other end of the corridor? So you don't get trapped in the flames?"

"I don't know."

Alice frowns. It doesn't sound like much of a plan. Brock's eyes are wide open and the scales on his face are practically standing up. She can tell he's desperate.

"Can't we put out the fire?" she says.

"The fire suppression system is down."

"Can we get there any other way?" Elias asks.

"No, this is the only way through the ship."

"What about outside the ship?"

Brock's reptilian eyes light up and, much to Alice's surprise, he laughs.

"You're smart, little Alonai," he says, patting Elias on the shoulder. "You might just have saved us all. Come on!"

Confused, Alice looks back and forth between Elias and Brock. What are they talking about? Outside the ship there's just empty space.

Brock sprints into a nearby corridor and they hurry behind him. Soon they come to a smaller room where the walls are lined with boxes. Straight ahead is another metal door. Strange how many doors there are on a spaceship. But this is the biggest Alice has seen so far. Next to the gate are various buttons and levers.

"This is the midship airlock," says Brock. "I can go outside and get into the aft airlock next to the engine room, where the central computer is. I just need a space suit."

He pulls out a box and picks up a large plastic cube.

"An emergency suit will have to do."

He presses the cube against his chest and the plastic appears to melt and mold around his body. Within seconds, it has completely enveloped him. The plastic is white, except over his head where it forms a transparent bubble.

"Stay here," says Brock. "I'll be back as soon as I've restarted the computer."

"No," Alice says firmly. "Don't you dare leave us here like a couple of kids."

She doesn't know where her courage is coming from, defying the ship's captain, but she can't bear the thought of sitting here and doing nothing.

Brock looks from her to Elias and back again. She can swear his eyes are smiling behind the transparent bubble.

"But you are kids."

"But, but…" Alice's mind races. She doesn't know why, but she simply must go with him.

"What if the Krao board and take us while you're gone?"

The scales around Brock's face rise and his eyes open wide. That thought had apparently not occurred to him. Alice continues:

"Besides, you may need more smart ideas in the engine room. Then you'll be glad you brought us along."

Brock chuckles.

"Fine, fine, we don't have time to chit chat. Here!"

He quickly takes two more plastic cubes from his box and pushes one against Elias' chest and the other against hers. The plastic starts to wrap around her body and she only just manages to stifle her surprise. Elias looks on in fascination as the plastic envelopes him.

Brock takes a steel rope and a small rocket out of another box. Alice once saw a similar rocket in a video online. Some maniac was flying around with it on his back. Then he crashed into a lake. This one looks more sophisticated.

Brock pushes the rocket against his shoulder, it melds into the plastic of the emergency suit and slides on its own into the middle of his wide back.

"Into the airlock!"

There must be headphones in the suit because Alice hears his voice clearly.

The door opens, sliding sideways, and they rush into the cramped space on the other side. There's another door. Brock closes it behind them and pushes a button. It feels a bit like standing in an elevator. Except in a space suit. There's a humming noise all around them.

"What's happening?" she says, trying to keep her voice steady.

"The air is being sucked out," says Elias. "Behind the next door is good ole space. We're going out for a wander through the stars!"

His eyes light up and Alice sighs… but some of her little brother's enthusiasm is rubbing off on her. This is pretty cool.

The space suits have big loops at the waist. Brock pulls the steel rope through his loop then attaches one end to Alice's and the other end to Elias's.

"Now you're attached to me. Whatever you do, don't detach the rope. Understood? I don't want to have to explain to Syndra why I let you drift away and disappear into the fathomless abyss."

He turns around and pulls a lever. The outer port opens. Beyond is nothing but space and stars.

"Six minutes before the boarding force arrives," says Brock. "Let's go!"

He launches himself into space.

"So…"

But Alice doesn't have time to say any more, because the rope tightens and she and Elias are pulled out after Brock into the great void.

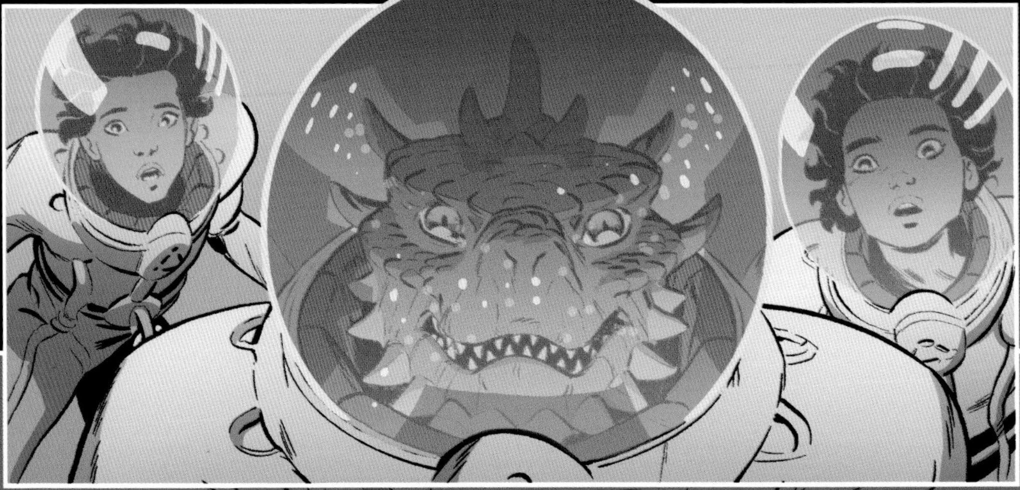
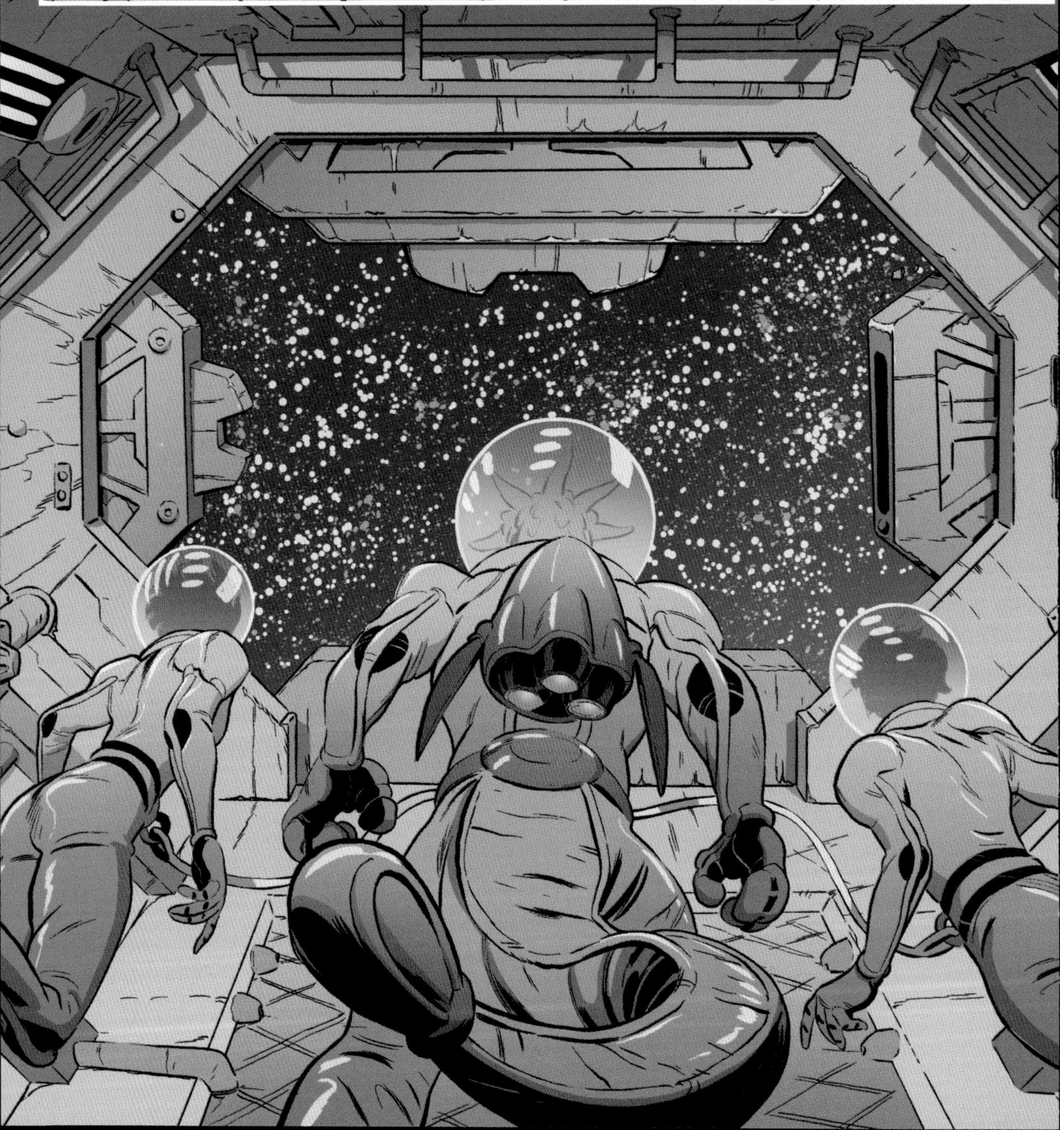

ELIAS

They spin around each other slowly. All around them are stars – glowing, flashing, vibrant stars. Elias has never seen anything like this. They look nothing like they do from Earth. From the ground he's seen only a pale imitation of starlight. Out here, it's like they're glowing just for him.

Then he remembers the Krao. They'll be here soon and he has to move now.

Though it's hard to think of anything horrible when he's surrounded by such marvels. He wants to enjoy it, just a moment longer.

He looks around, taking it in. He'll never forget this. Then he sighs and takes a deep breath. He's ready.

Brock pulls both of them towards him, putting one arm around each of them. Then he lights the rocket on his back. Blue flames shoot out.

They rush through the nothingness like a glowing comet with a blazing tail. Now Alice is laughing. If there's anything she loves, it's high speed. Elias smiles.

He hasn't seen any controls on the rocket, but Brock still

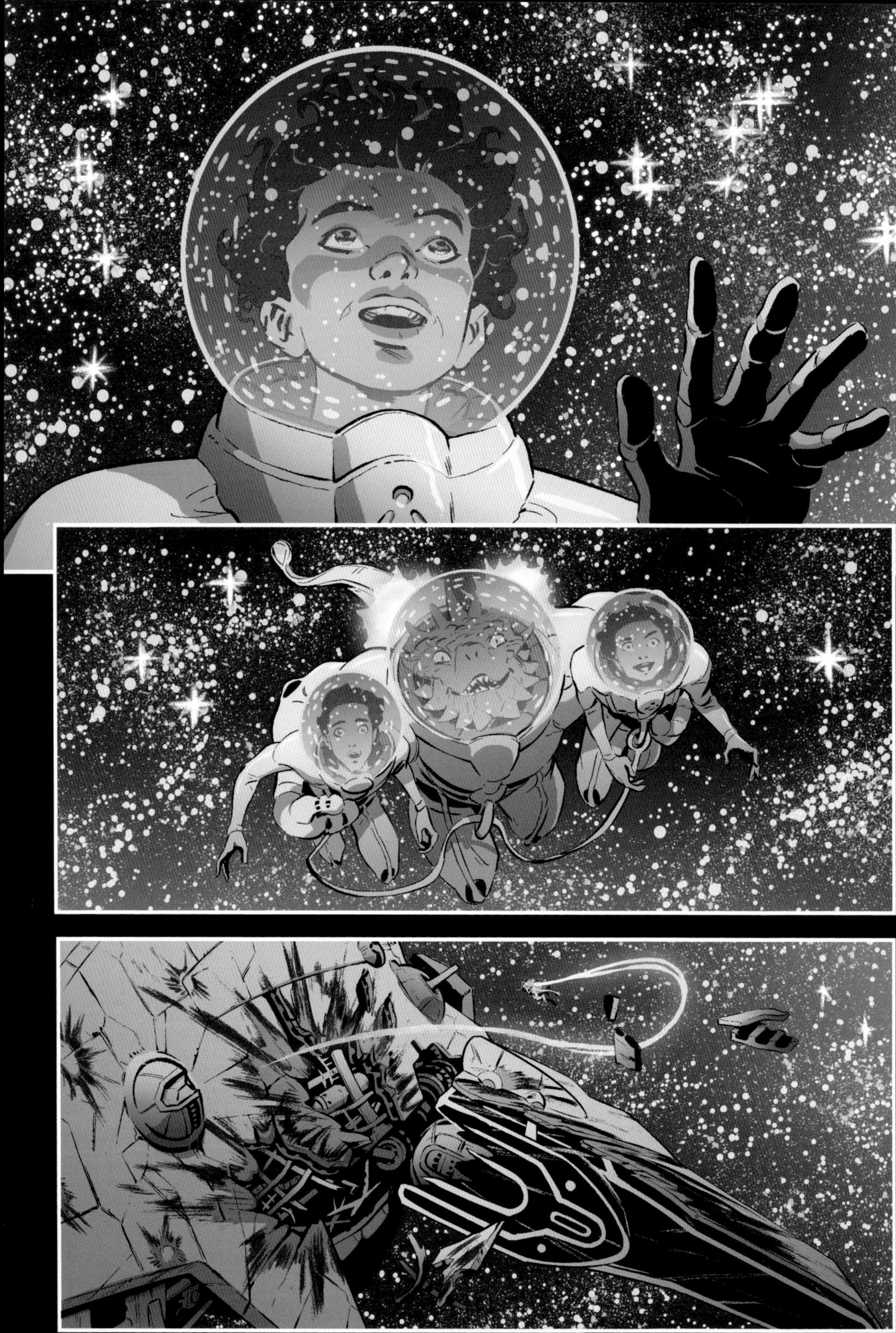

seems to be able to steer it somehow. Next to them, the hull of the Phoenix rushes past at a furious pace. The ship has smooth lines, but is also sharp and angular in places. They pass by a large, shapeless hole. The metal bent into strange shapes, black and burnt. That must be where the torpedo hit.

They move at high speed towards the rear of the ship, towards the huge engines. Suddenly Brock turns a somersault, spinning his body around. He dives feet first and brakes hard with the rocket. Elias feels himself start to slip out of Brock's grip and his stomach clenches in terror. Then they stop. Brock has calculated the braking perfectly and their landing is smooth. They stop right in front of an airlock. Inside, the engine room must be close by.

"Three minutes," Brock growls, opening a small hatch and pressing a code on a control panel.

And they enter.

ELIAS

Brock bursts into a huge hall full of big machines. He doesn't even stop to detach the rope. He drops the rocket mid-run. Elias has to run as fast as he can to avoid being dragged through the room on his heels. He barely has time to look around. The hall and everything in it passes in a blur.

Another door is torn open and they enter a new room filled from top to bottom with black cubes. They're stacked on top of each other in steel racks with red and blue lights glowing and flashing all around. In the middle of the floor is a large computer terminal. Brock bends over it and starts pressing claws on the buttons.

After a few seconds he stops.

"It's not accepting my password!" he growls.

"What do you mean?" Elias says.

"As captain, I have a master password to open all systems, but the central computer is refusing to restart Arisa. It requires a code I don't have!"

Their headphones crackle. It's Syndra.

"Brock, can you hear me?"

"Yes, I'm here."

"I can see them now, the Krao boarding force. They've stopped their shuttle outside and are approaching in space suits. They have tools and weapons with them. They'll start hacking the front airlock in one minute."

Elias feels a rush of fear move through his body.

"I'm at the central computer," replies Brock, "but I can't restart Arisa! It requires a code I don't know. My password doesn't work." He points his claw at some symbols on the screen. "It says the code was set when Arisa was installed. Who did that?"

Syndra groans.

"Guess."

"Parishvi."

"Mom!" says Elias. "Does she have the code?"

Brock just sighs.

"You have 30 seconds!" says Syndra.

Elias starts jumping up and down. He can't help it. His heart is pounding so hard that it might burst out of his chest.

"There's a clue here," says Brock, "but I don't understand it. It says..." He clears his throat. "The Phoenix travels through space at night."

"What did you say?" says Alice. Her eyes are wide open.

"The Phoenix floats through space at night."

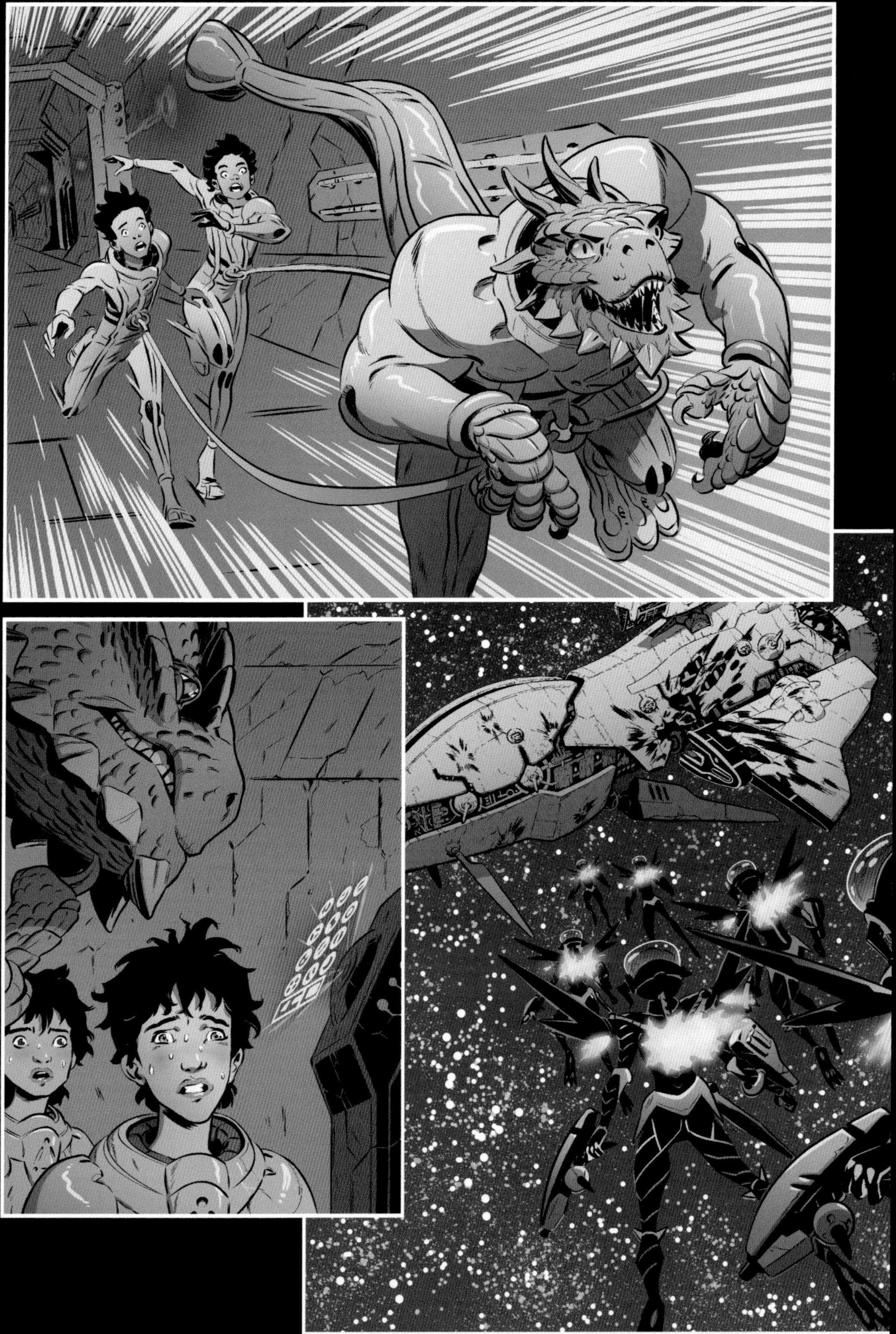

Then Elias understands. Something clicks in his brain and all the pieces fall into place.

"The lullaby!" he shouts. "Press, let's see… 'Seven came'. Start with seven."

"No!" Alice shouts even louder. "It starts with 'It has five horns on its head'. Press five!"

"Five," Brock repeats, touching the screen.

Elias starts to sing. He knows this song inside out.

"Sleep my two and enjoy her journey."

"Two!" Alice and Brock shout at the same time.

Elias continues.

"Let the dream come true. Seven came. Two came. Four sheep came. Let's count them. Three came. Five came. Eight sheep came. Manna rains from heaven."

"Eight," Brock mumbles, and presses the last symbol with his big claw. Hundreds of small green lights turn on and bathe the entire room in color. "It worked!"

Elias looks around with wide eyes. He can hardly believe it's true.

Arisa's voice projects from the ceiling.

"Initiating neural network. Loading personality matrix. Connecting to all nodes. Complete. How may I help you?"

Brock raises his hands and roars in triumph.

"Arisa! So infinitely wonderful to have you back."

"Nice to see you too, Captain."

Then there is a crackle in the speaker again.

"They've opened the outer door of the airlock!" screams Syndra.

"Arisa," says Brock. "As you can see, we have some unwelcome guests."

"I see them, they are inside the front airlock. They have closed the outer port and are working on the inner port. I estimate they will unlock it within 37 seconds."

"Start the engines! The Phoenix needs full power."

"Aye, Captain."

Through the door to the large hall, Elias sees the entire engine room bathed in light. There's a banging sound and purple flashes fly from the huge engines. He briefly wonders if the engines are broken, but then he glances at Brock. The captain is watching the activity in the engine room with a big happy grin on his face, so everything must be working as it should.

"But the Krao!" says Elias. "They're already in!"

Brock's smile becomes sharp somehow, almost unpleasant.

"Arisa. Close all security doors throughout the Phoenix, except the one at the front airlock. Then open both airlock ports."

"Roger."

Suddenly a holo-screen appears and Elias sees half a dozen figures in black space suits crowded into the Phoenix's airlock. They're armed with weapons and equipment. One of them has some kind of data device and is trying to break into the electronic lock. Then the inner port opens. The figures raise their weapons, ready to storm the ship. But then the port behind them opens as well.

The Krao barely have time to glance over their shoulder before the ship's atmosphere rushes towards them like a violent gust of wind and throws them out of the lock. Helplessly they swirl away, into the great void.

"Close the ports."

"Roger."

"Nicely done," Syndra says in their headphones. "You sure know how to take care of unwelcome guests, Captain."

"Their shuttle has already begun work on salvaging the boarding force," says Arisa. "But it's a complicated job. They won't be returning to the Phoenix anytime soon."

They did it! They won! No one was going to take the Phoenix and no one was going to kidnap them. And it was their code that had saved them. Mom's code.

"Raise the shields," says Brock. "And full speed on the engine. We are in no position to fight right now."

"Aye, Captain."

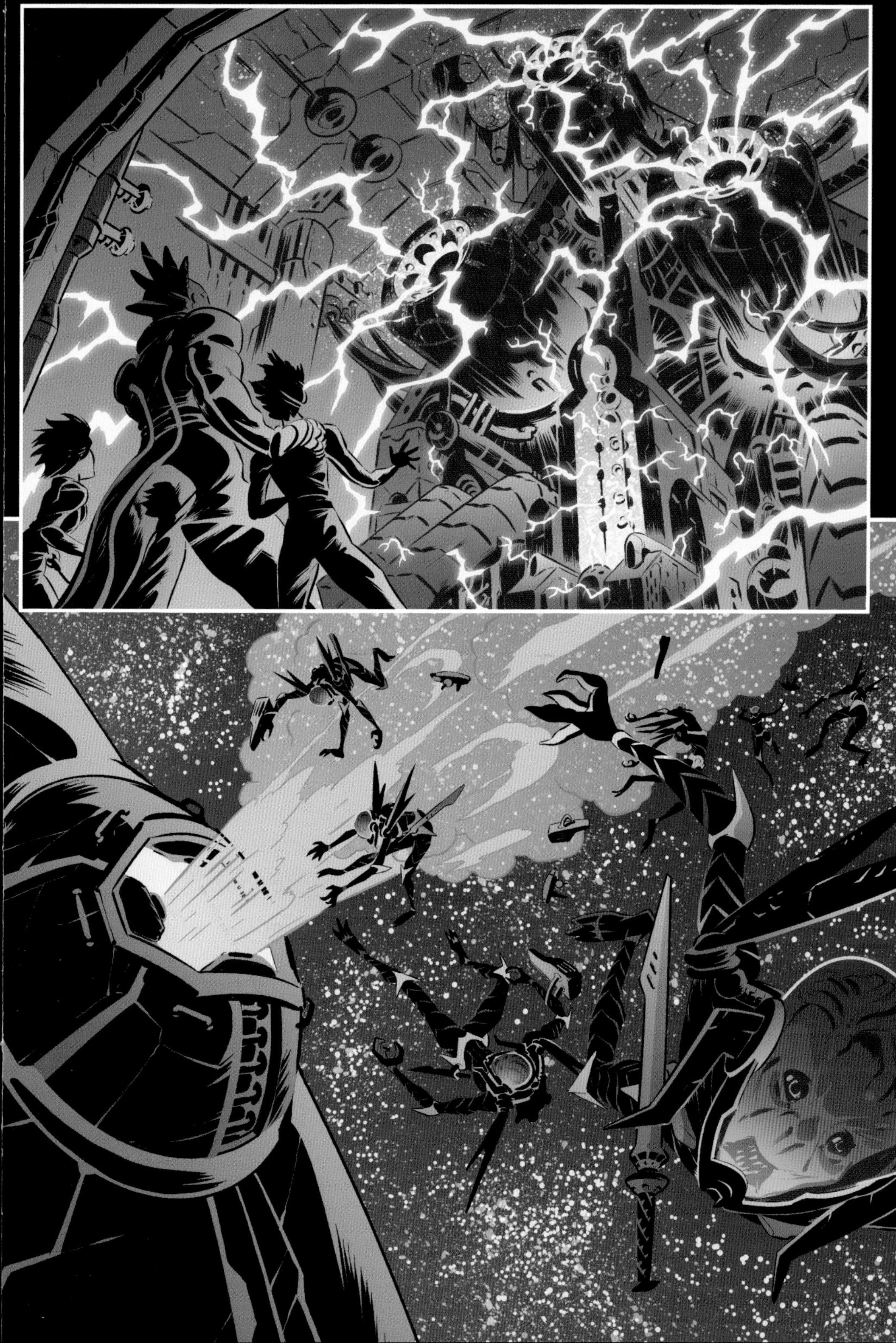

"And send drones to repair the hole in the mid-section at once."

"Already on the way."

Brock slumps onto the floor.

"Thank you," he says, looking first at Alice and then at Elias. "If it weren't for you two, all would've been lost. This actually reminds me of some of the wild adventures we went on with Parishvi. You are indeed your mother's children."

Alice looks tired but pleased. She sits down next to Brock and takes a few deep breaths. Elias follows their example. A strange wave of joy rises inside him. He knows that he shouldn't feel this way while Mom is still a prisoner. But he's grateful for having escaped and motivated more than ever to find Mom. A big smile spreads across his face.

Alice nudges the big lizard on his side with her elbow.

"Didn't I say you might need more smart ideas?"

Brock snorts.

"You did indeed."

"We did only what we could," Elias says.

"And you did well."

Then they go quiet. They sit there, catching their breath, each immersed in their own thoughts. Elias can't help but hum the last lines of the lullaby.

No one can see the future

Keep the song inside you
No, no one can see the future
Keep the song inside you.

ALICE

Alice and Elias follow Brock out through the engine room doors and find themselves in a corridor. They've taken off their space suits. Arisa has announced that Farei will survive, but the big bird is still asleep. Brock wants to check on her then go straight to the bridge to steer the Phoenix to safety. The engines are at full speed and the entire ship vibrates as they zoom away from the enemy vessel.

"Isn't it amazing?" Elias exclaims.

"What?" Alice asks.

"The lullaby! Mom hid the passcode to the central computer in our lullaby! Don't you understand what that means?"

Alice is in no mood for guessing games. Too much has happened. And even though Mom has helped save the Phoenix somehow, she can't forget her betrayal. If Mom were here now, she would hug her and yell at her at the same time.

"I give up," she mumbles. "What?"

Elias groans.

"She knew we would need it someday! She knew that we might end up on the Phoenix!"

Alice tries to look at the situation through Elias' eyes; the lullaby as a wonderful secret key. But the only thing she can think of is how Mom kept the truth from them, year after year after year. Not just from them, but from Dad too.

Poor Dad. He still has no idea who he is really married to. "She lied to us."

"No! She didn't lie! She just didn't tell the whole truth," says Elias, just like last time.

"We're not even human!" cries Alice. "Have you thought about that? We are half something else, half Alonai. She lied about that too!"

She feels like punching something. Suddenly she misses her training sword. If only she had it, she would... She's not sure what she would do, but she wouldn't feel so damn defenseless.

She pictures Mom standing before her in her fencing jacket, gloves, leg protectors and mask, sword in one hand and a parrying dagger in the other. She sees her demonstrating a simple fight sequence in exaggeratedly slow movements before going on to more advanced exercises. She moves smoothly across the lawn and increases her tempo until the sword is swooshing around her. She stops, lowers her arms and smiles. Mom. Alice wants to cry.

In the same second, the Phoenix hurdles to the side and Alice almost runs straight into the corridor wall.

Then Arisa's voice is heard, calm and factual:

"The enemy has fired several missiles at us."

"Are the shields up?" says Brock.

"I'm sorry, but the shield systems are not yet properly activated. They need more time."

"Time we don't have," muttered Brock. "The missiles can't be allowed to hit us! If they do, it's all over."

"I guarantee I will try to avoid them to the best of my ability."

There is a dull thud and the Phoenix lurches again. The whole ship sings, like a struck church bell. Alice feels tears burning behind her eyelids. Not another attack. She can't take it.

"Hold on." says Arisa. "I have to push the engines to the max and the gravitational fields are not yet fully functional. I won't be able to compensate."

"What's she talking about?" Elias asks with concern in his voice. "What should we hold on to?"

"This!" says Brock, grabbing hold of a handle on the wall that Alice hadn't noticed before. Looking around, she realizes that there are strategically placed handles all along the corridor. Brock quickly throws an arm around Elias and holds on to him.

"Alice," he shouts. "Grab a handle!"

She leaps over to the other side and grabs a handle opposite Brock and Elias.

"With both hands!" shouts the big lizard.

Alice takes a firm hold, and not a second too soon, because the very next moment a strong force tries to suck her back down the corridor. It's like sitting in a super-fast car speeding up the motorway, only worse. Her feet slip and slide on the floor. She blinks and everything starts to tilt. The corridor ahead of them is slanting upwards like a see-saw, and behind them the floor is sloping down. The corridor has been transformed into a slide. Her fingers ache and she wonders what would happen if she lost her grip and fell down on the closed engine room door. She would get hurt, of course. But just how much injury can the nanites heal?

She has no desire to find out. She grits her teeth and tries to ignore the pain in her hands.

Elias looks up and down the sloping corridor in confusion. He's safe with Brock holding on to him.

"What's going on?!" he shouts.

"The Phoenix is accelerating as fast as the engines can tolerate," Brock says. He's hanging casually with one hand on the handle and balancing his feet against the sloping floor. He looks completely unfazed, like he could hang

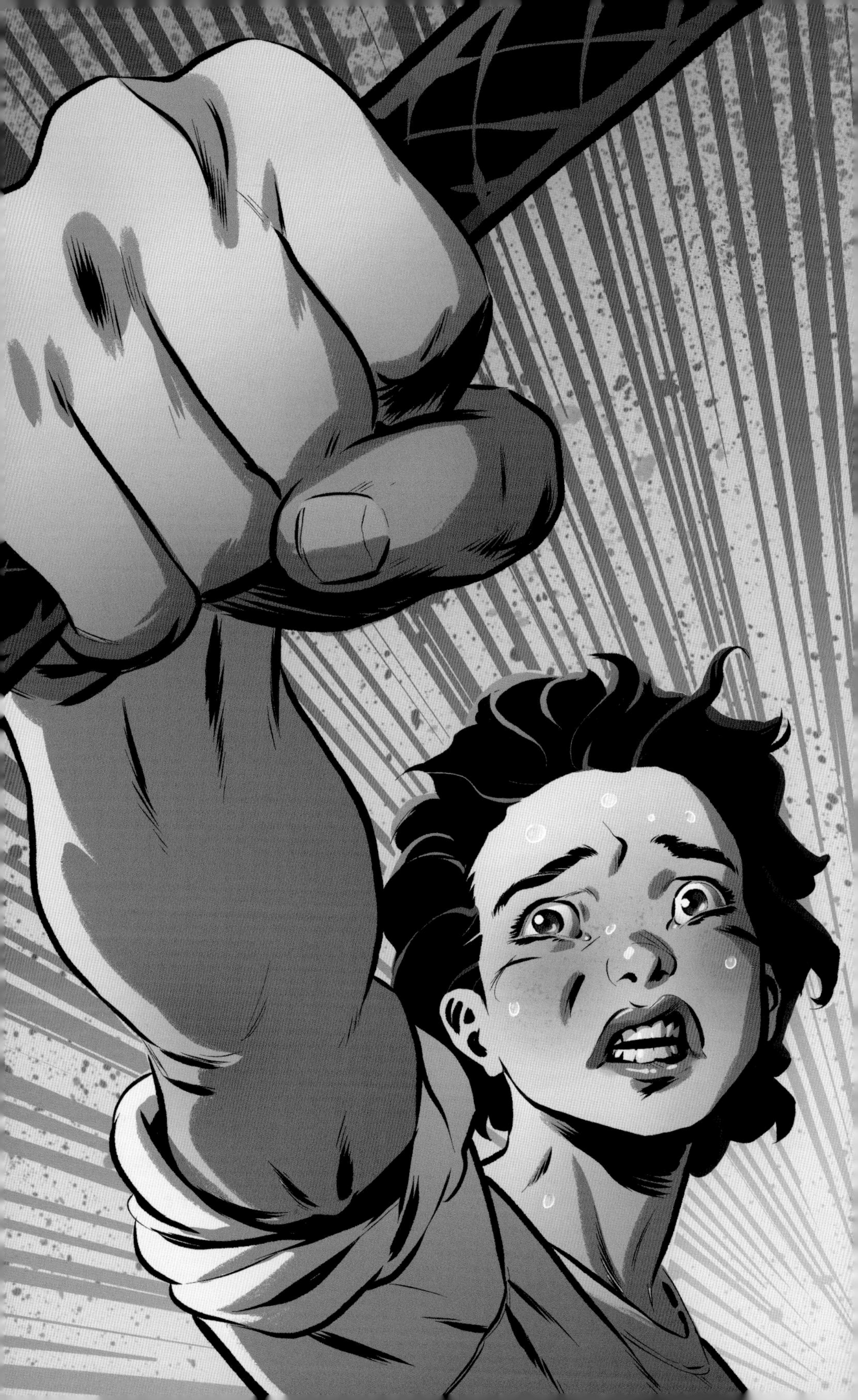

there for eternity. "As the ship pushes forward, we're pushed backwards."

"I don't give a damn about the physics!" screams Alice. "I can barely feel my fingers!"

"I'm sorry if this is causing any discomfort," says Arisa. "But I guarantee it would be even more unpleasant to be blasted into subatomic particles by enemy missiles."

Well, obviously.

Alice tries to hold on, but she can feel herself getting heavier and heavier, as if an octopus with long tentacles has gripped her around the waist and is pulling harder and harder. Her fingers go numb.

Then it happens... one of her hands loses its grip. She is going to fall!

"Stop!" she roars.

Brock suddenly looks worried.

"Arisa! Can you lower..." he begins but doesn't finish.

"The enemy has stopped shooting," says Arisa. "Their weapons can no longer reach us. We are safe."

In an instant, the corridor tips back to normal and Alice drops to the floor. The impact knocks the wind out of her. Her arms ache terribly and she can barely straighten her fingers. Brock, on the other hand, lands as agilely as a cat. He sets Elias down, who immediately rushes over to Alice.

"Are you OK?"

This is all just too much. She lashes out with her arms. "Leave me alone!"

She immediately regrets it when she sees the pain in her little brother's face.

"Sorry," she says, slowly rising to her feet. "Come here."

She gives him a long hug.

"That's OK," he says. "Arisa says we're safe now. The Krao can't reach us. Come on. We have to keep moving. Farei is waiting for us."

BROCK

SYNDRA

FAREI

ARISA

ALICE

ELIAS

ELIAS

Alice seems tired and angry. Elias doesn't really know what to do about it. Maybe there's nothing to do. He would love for her to experience this journey the same way as he does and enjoy at least a little bit all the awesome stuff that surrounds them.

They arrive at a door and Brock hesitates.

"I've put out the fire. You can pass now," says Arisa.

"Good," Brock says, pushing it open.

They step into a soot-covered mess. So this is the corridor where the fire raged. Elias breathes in the acrid smell. He hears Alice grunt. There's a huge hole in one side of the metal wall, the edges melted inwards. Elias peers through the hole into another room: scraps and warped remains are scattered all over the floor. The far wall of the room has also been blasted away, leaving a gaping hole. Elias shudders at the realization that he's staring straight into space. He can see the stars.

"But, but…" he says, pointing.

"But what?" says Brock.

"There's a hole! How are we breathing right now? Why isn't all the air rushing out?"

"An emergency field is holding the oxygen in," Brock says. "It is a kind of force field that is automatically activated if the ship is punctured. Emergency fields have been around for a long time. It's nothing special."

Nothing special for Brock maybe…

Elias can't take his eyes off the stars. Then he sees a small beetle-shaped robot crawling around the opening. It moves its large jaws toward the hull and starts to flash. Then another beetle comes, and another, and another, until the hole is swarming with them. Alice is staring in fascination too. She likes insects. And these are actually similar to her African beetles at home. Except that the robots are much bigger, of course, and made of metal.

"Good," says Brock. "The drones are in place. They'll fix the damage in no time."

"So cool!" says Elias.

Alice nods and seems to relax a little.

"What room was this?" she asks Brock. "Before it was reduced to ashes."

"Our hobby room."

"Hobby room?"

"It can take a long time to travel from star to star. Sometimes you need a way to pass the time. We had books in here, proper paper books, I mean. That's where Farei kept her meditation globes," he says, pointing, "and over there Syndra had her light sculptures and virtual game consoles. She plays with Kapa sometimes. He likes gaming too." He opens his eyes wide. "Kapa!"

"He's still hibernating," says Arisa from the ceiling. Brock laughs.

"So typical of him. The whole ship is incapacitated, we nearly got boarded and he sleeps through it all. But if I remember correctly, his hibernation will soon be over. Tell me when he wakes up."

"Roger."

Brock beats his tail on the floor twice in quick succession, sending ash flying, then sets off through the corridors with purposeful strides. Elias and Alice follow close behind.

"Arisa! Just before that torpedo hit us, we scanned the enemy ship. Was that data lost or saved?"

"It's saved," says Arisa. "It is definitely a Krao ship. However, I cannot determine whether it is Madukar. They have blasted off the name engraving from the stern."

"So that no one can identify them," Brock mutters. "I don't like this."

"As far as life forms are concerned, we discovered…" Arisa allows a long pause, "… 1,553 Krao and one Alonai."

"Is it Mom?" Alice asks in a flash.

"It is impossible to say based on the data collected," says Arisa.

"But who else could it be?" says Elias.

"She said herself in her message that they'd captured her!"

"It's impossible to say," Arisa repeats.

"But it seems likely," says Brock, "and it's the best lead we have."

"We have to save her," says Elias.

"We will, little Alonai, rest assured."

They arrive at the sickbay.

Farei is lying unconscious on one of the bunks. Elias isn't

sure, but it may be the same bed that Alice lay in just a few hours ago, though it's changed to an oval shape, similar to a bird's nest. Wires stretch down from the ceiling and small metal electrodes are attached to Farei's head. Syndra bends over her with a monitoring device in hand.

"How is she?" Brock asks.

He gets a weak smile in response.

"Her brain looks good. There shouldn't be any permanent damage."

Elias breathes a sigh of relief.

Farei is going to be OK.

Then the monitor beeps and Syndra opens her eyes wide.

"She's waking up!" she says.

A filmy membrane slides away from Farei's eyes. She blinks and focuses. Brock takes a step closer and he's the first thing she sees. She tries to sit up with a jerk, but she can barely lift her head from the pillow.

"Oh, Captain. I'm so sorry. It was a torpedo. Camouflaged. Old empire technology. I didn't see it until it was too late. "

Brock takes her hand in his and pats her long, curved talons affectionately.

"Don't worry about it. We're alive. The ship pulled through." He nods to Elias and Alice. "Our young Alonai are alive and well."

Farei collapses on the bed.

"I want to apologize anyway."

Brock nods.

"Then I accept your apology. I know you won't make the same mistake again."

Farei's eyes blaze.

"Never."

"Captain," Arisa says from the ceiling. "I just want to alert you that the enemy ship is on a new course away from us. I think they're going to jump into hyperspace. We may risk losing them."

Brock and Syndra scramble to the bridge. Elias and Alice aren't far behind. Elias sinks into his seat. Do they have to run all the time? His legs have turned to jelly.

Alice, on the other hand, seems to be having a hard time standing still. She rocks back and forth, shifting one foot to the other, transfixed by the holo-screen. It shows the large, jagged contours of the enemy ship turning away from the Phoenix, and turning away from Earth.

"They're leaving," says Syndra. "Are they giving up?"

"It seems so," says Brock. "They realized they could never catch us. Though they're large and well-armed, they aren't fast. We are." The ship on the screen speeds up, its vast engine working hard to drive it out of the solar system. There's an explosion of light and suddenly, the ship is gone.

"They've gone to hyperspace," says Syndra.

"Did we get good vector data on their hyperspace jump?" Brock asks.

Syndra stares down at her computer terminal. Elias strains his neck to get a glimpse. Strange symbols and graphs dance on the screen.

"Pretty good," she says. "We know roughly in which direction they are travelling."

"Roughly?" says Brock, obviously dissatisfied.

"There's a space station that way. It's a trading station, the last known old empire outpost in these parts."

"What's it called?"

"Aertro's outpost."

"Which one?"

"Number 34. The Iron Rose."

Brock snorts and his tail winds into a coil. He looks like he has just eaten a lemon. Or whatever sour equivalent a space lizard might eat.

"The Iron Rose," says Brock emphatically. "That could very well be their destination. Since the fall of the empire, it has become a safe haven for smugglers, pirates, opportunists, and vagrants."

A grunt rises deep in his throat. "Plot a route. We're going to pay a visit!"

Syndra nods, pushes a few buttons on her control panel

and the Phoenix makes a sharp turn. Elias hears the powerful engines working, deep down in the hull.

"Hyperspace coordinates entered," says Arisa.

Elias opens his eyes wide. This is it! They're not only about to leave Earth, but they're about to leave the entire solar system, and voyage out among the stars. Who knows what might await them out there.

"Jump!" shouts Brock.

Space implodes around them as the Phoenix plunges into hyperspace, towards a space station called the Iron Rose, and after the ship where their mother is held captive.

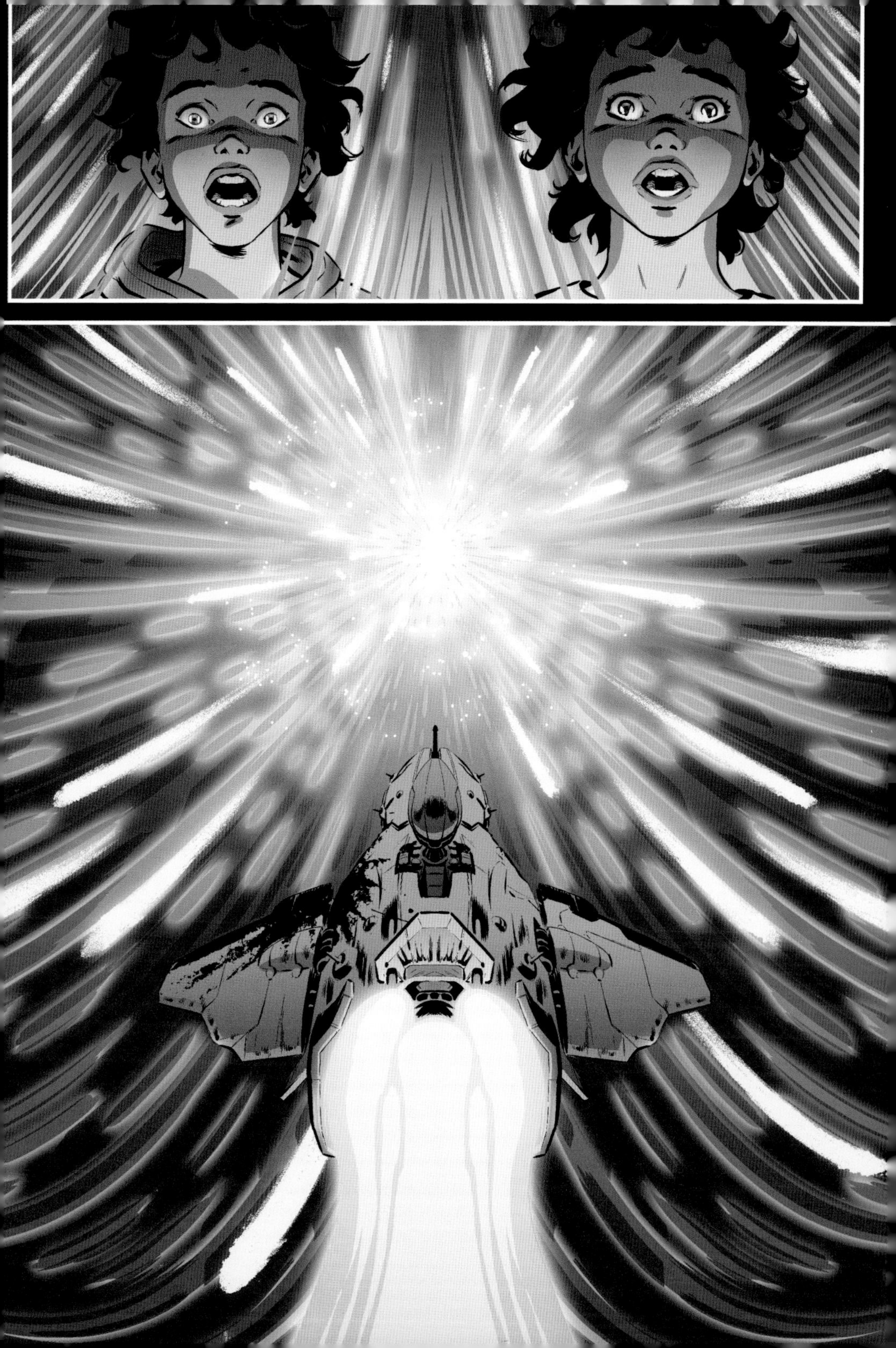

THE PHOENIX

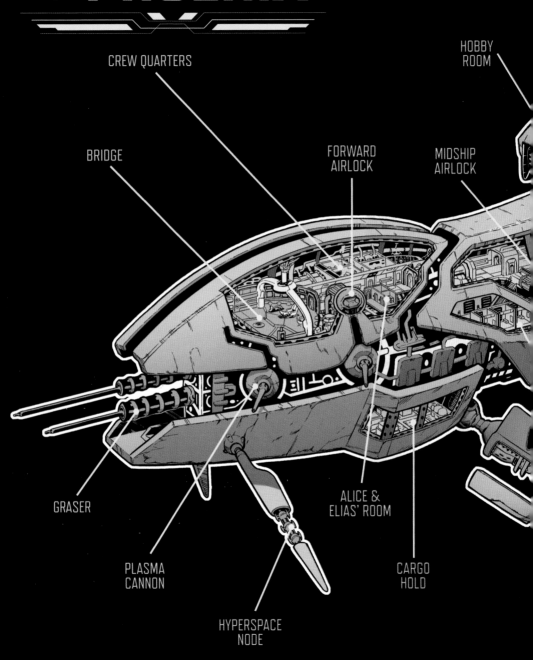

CREW QUARTERS

HOBBY ROOM

BRIDGE

FORWARD AIRLOCK

MIDSHIP AIRLOCK

GRASER

ALICE & ELIAS' ROOM

PLASMA CANNON

CARGO HOLD

HYPERSPACE NODE

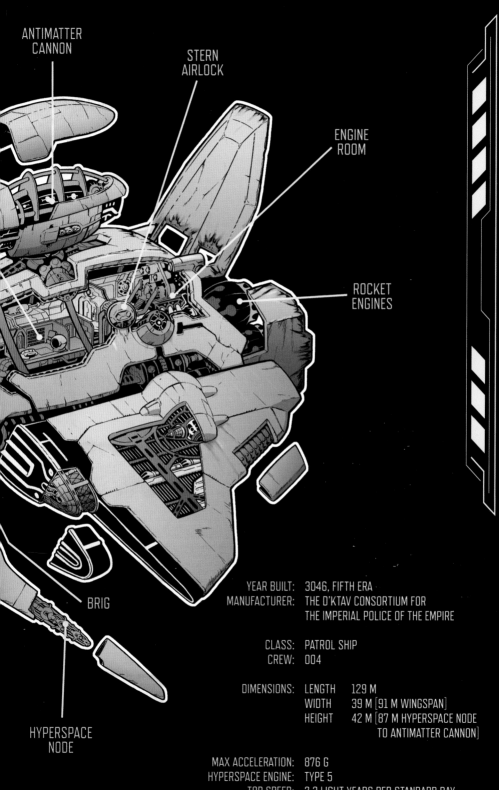

ANTIMATTER
CANNON

STERN
AIRLOCK

ENGINE
ROOM

ROCKET
ENGINES

BRIG

HYPERSPACE
NODE

YEAR BUILT: 3046, FIFTH ERA
MANUFACTURER: THE D'KTAV CONSORTIUM FOR
THE IMPERIAL POLICE OF THE EMPIRE

CLASS: PATROL SHIP
CREW: 004

DIMENSIONS: LENGTH   129 M
WIDTH   39 M [91 M WINGSPAN]
HEIGHT   42 M [87 M HYPERSPACE NODE
TO ANTIMATTER CANNON]

MAX ACCELERATION: 876 G
HYPERSPACE ENGINE: TYPE 5
TOP SPEED: 2.3 LIGHT YEARS PER STANDARD DAY

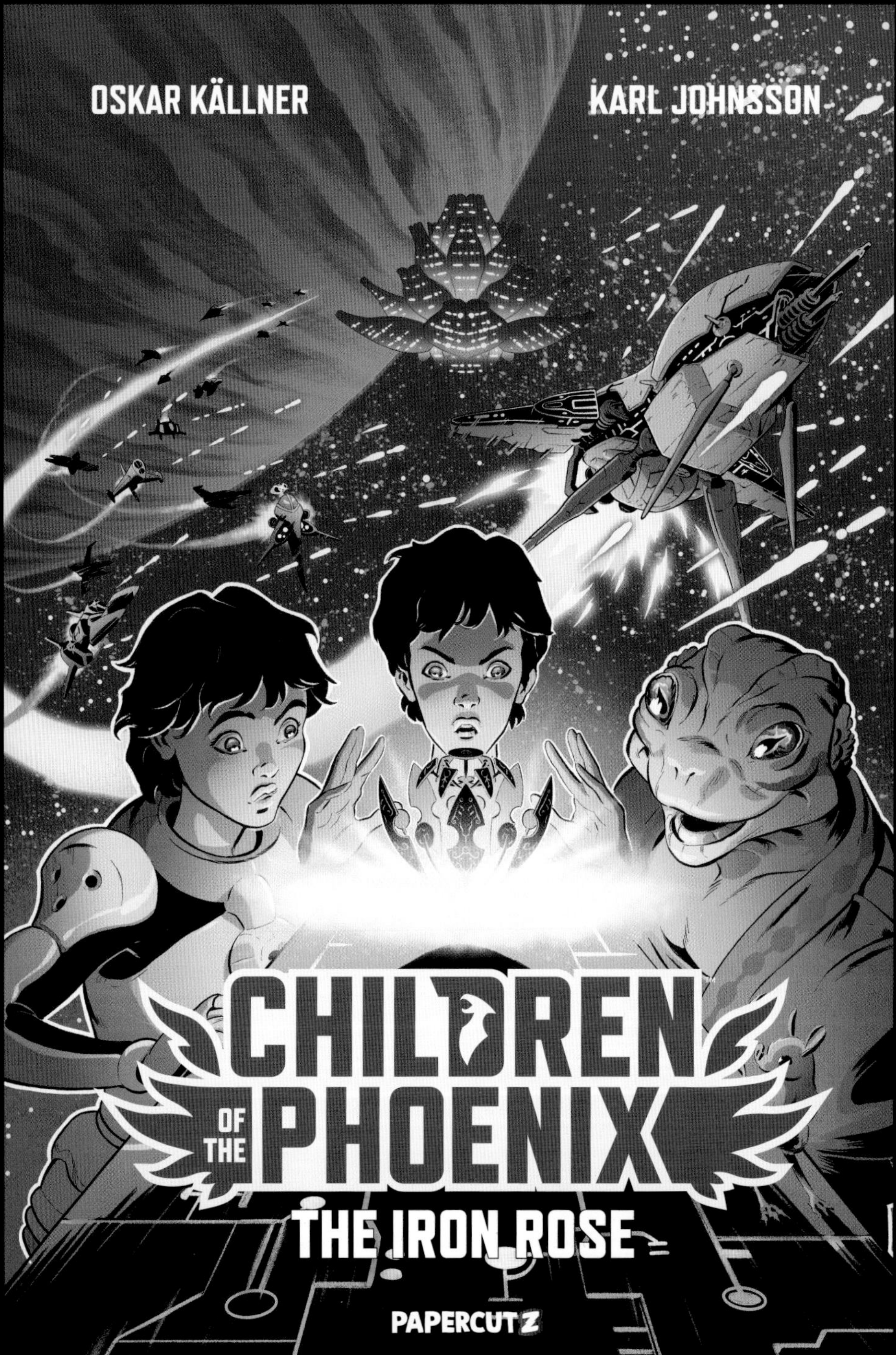
OSKAR KÄLLNER
KARL JOHNSSON
CHILDREN OF THE PHOENIX
THE IRON ROSE
PAPERCUTZ